Praise for
TO WONDER AND STARSHINE

"Jendia Gammon spins tales of magic, mystery, and beautiful weirdness! This collection shows the range and passion she brings to each of her stories." —Jonathan Maberry, *New York Times* bestselling author of *NecroTek: Cold War* and *Red Empire*

"*To Wonder and Starshine* is a gorgeous tapestry of magical tales for the young (and young at heart!). With her trademark lyrical prose, deft plotting, and engaging characterization Jendia Gammon once again establishes herself as a master-storyteller, crafting a book to be cherished for generations. Highly recommended!" —D.K. (Danika) Stone, bestselling multi-genre author of the Waterton trilogy, *Inescapable*, *All the Feels*, and *Switchback*

"*To Wonder and Starshine* is a frolic though space, time, and different realms. Once again, Gammon delivers a book bursting with colour that dares minds to dream bigger, search farther, and imagine more vividly. You'll be left believing in goodness and wonder in the world." —Jesse Reid, author of *Bran Finds His Feathers*

"Jendia Gammon weaves nature, technology, and magic into an enchanting collection of stories with the charm of fairytale and the heft of modern myth." —Gareth L. Powell, author of *Future's Edge* and *Embers of Water*

"These glimpses beyond the everyday are so lovingly crafted." —Eddie Robson, author of *Drunk on All Your Strange New Words*

Praise for

THE SHADOW GALAXY

(by Jendia Gammon writing as J. Dianne Dotson)

"A sharply entertaining collection spanning all corners of the genre, filled with horrors and wonders and acutely human moments." — Adrian Tchaikovsky, author of *Children of Time*

"A deeply satisfying collection of fantasies that ranges from Americana to outer space, charming and precise in equal measure." — Paul Cornell, author of *Witches of Lychford* and *I Walk with Monsters*

"There truly is a story for everyone in this collection of stories. If you haven't found one yet, then keep reading!" —Blaise Ancona, Under the Radar SFF Books

TO WONDER AND STARSHINE

JENDIA GAMMON

TREPIDATIO
PUBLISHING

ISBN: 978-1-68510-158-9 (trade paper)
ISBN: 978-1-68510-159-6 (ebook)
Library of Congress Catalog Number: 2025942267

First printing edition: July 25, 2025
Printed by Trepidatio Publishing in the United States of America.
Edited by Sean Leonard
Proofreading and Interior Layout by Scarlett R. Algee

Trepidatio Publishing, an imprint of JournalStone Publishing
1400 North Wood Rd.
Murphysboro, Illinois 62966

Trepidatio books may be ordered through booksellers or by contacting:
JournalStone | www.journalstone.com

BOOKS BY JENDIA GAMMON

As Jendia Gammon:

To Wonder and Starshine
Atacama
Doomflower

Coming soon:
Dungeon Crawl at the Haunted Mall: A Choose Your Own Adventure Book (2026)
Godfestation (2026)
The Vale of Seven Dragons (2026)
Coursers of Wings and Flame (2027)
The Vale of Fire Wrought (2028)

As J. Dianne Dotson:

The Inn at the Amethyst Lantern (Nebula and BSFA Award Finalist)
The Shadow Galaxy: A Collection of Short Stories and Poetry

The Questrison Saga:
Heliopause: The Questrison Saga: Book One
Ephemeris: The Questrison Saga: Book Two
Accretion: The Questrison Saga: Book Three
Luminiferous: The Questrison Saga: Book Four

Coming soon:
The Secret of the Sapphire Sentinel (2025)
The Dawn of Dusk and Twilight (2026)

For my family.
And for anyone who's got their head in the clouds or among the stars...this one's for you.

CONTENTS

TO WONDER AND STARSHINE

ELPH AND THE GREEN FAIRY

ELPH STARED OPEN-MOUTHED at the crevice in the moss-covered rocks, bright chartreuse after recent rain, where his short wooden sword had fallen. He had swung it around his head and somehow released it, and off it had spun, right down into the shady depths, out of sight. He ran his hands through his spiky ginger hair and whistled a note of frustration. Mum would be furious, he knew; Uncle Geoff had given him that sword a year prior. Elph had worn its hilt down from much play and practice. He stared down at his traitorous, callused hands. How could he have let it go? The crevice was too narrow to climb through, and he was unsure where it led: a cave? He was not dressed for spelunking, with his dark green wool sweater, patched at the elbows and fraying at the wrists; tan cargo shorts; long, striped docks that drooped on his thin legs; and dew-soaked tennis shoes. He looked up and around, and beyond the boulders he could see the entangled canopy of ancient oaks, their leaves budding in the longer days of spring. There was nothing for it: he'd have to go up or around and over those boulders somehow, or into that cluster of woods, and find that sword. Then he heard a little wail.

He blinked his light brown eyes and wondered if he'd imagined it.

But no: another wail. And it was high-pitched yet clipped. It sounded...irritated?

"Hello?" he called. "Who's there?"

At first, only the hissing and creaking of oak tree boughs met his ears. And then, quite clearly, he heard, "Hmmph!"

Elph shoved his hands in his pockets and rocked back and forth where he stood. On the one hand, he reasoned, if it were someone dangerous, he'd know by now. And they wouldn't sound like a frustrated kid.

I could try to find them. Maybe they lost a sword too, he thought.

With a shrug, he made his way through new citrine-hued spring vines and young brambles and already leggy grasses, all of them dripping from the remnants of the morning fog that hung in the valley like a scarf knitted from raindrops. His shoes, their soles worn from much play on the concrete of his schoolyard, slipped and skidded over hidden stones. But by and by, he clambered around the cluster of boulders that had seemingly consumed his favorite toy and faced then a thicket of shrubs and vines surrounding the oaks. They were strange oaks to him: their tops all bent toward each other as if they huddled to whisper, and indeed that is what it sounded like they were doing, as the wind shivered its way through their gnarled branches. Beneath the bud-laden canopy, it looked to Elph like there must be a small, shady hollow, but he could not see its bottom.

Maybe there is *a cave.*

He shrugged again. He was there; why not go for it? So he pushed and pulled his way through the wild hedges surrounding the oak pocket and finally he fell right through—and slid on his bottom on the bank of a vernal pool. There at the edge of the pool, a feeble beam of sunlight shone in a long shaft, illuminating what at first looked like a girl perhaps his age, sitting with her arms wrapped around her knees, and scowling. But the light bent around her and spun, and the colors of the little being dazzled his eyes.

It *was* a girl. *Maybe.* But she was unlike any girl he had ever seen before, and her hair was wild and dark gold with hints of green, drifting as if she were underwater. Her skin shimmered pale gold, and her outfit looked made of nothing resembling fabric. Perhaps feathers, or cobwebs, or some indefinable material, but it shifted in hue along the entire range of hues from palest spring green to turquoise to deep twilight blue. Elph assumed that the chartreuse covering draped around her shoulders was some sort of cloak, but then she saw him and gasped, and that pale covering shot up like wings of a moth.

He stared at her.

She stared at him.

"You're—you're a fairy!" he shouted.

She frowned at him, and he noticed two little antennae on her forehead jerking straight up.

"You're a rude little boy," she hissed.

He gasped.

She stood and dusted herself off, and her outfit flickered and sparkled in all its cool hues. Her hair looked most mutinous, billowing in all directions. A little frown rested between her brows, and she lifted her pointy chin to stare down at him—or at least to act like it, for they were very close in height—in pure disdain.

"Why am I rude?" Elph cried.

"You threw a sword at me, didn't you?" she demanded.

Elph looked this way and that but did not see his sword.

"Where is it?" he shouted.

"See? Rude." She folded her arms and glared at him. "Not even an apology. I have done many things, little human, but none deserved the hurtling of a sword! Which, by the way, is rather coarse and provincial, don't you think?"

Elph felt his face go red and knew that probably his ginger eyebrows glowed pale orange yellow, a most unpleasant appearance, and that irritated him even more.

"It's *my sword*. Give it back!" He thrust his hand out. The vernal pool sat between them, still and pure and unaffected by their drama. The only movement in its glassy surface was the reflection of oaks in the wind above, and two crochety beings at its edge.

The fairy shrugged. "Can't."

"Why not?"

"Because I don't have it!"

Elph was really angry now. Fairy or not, that was his sword, and he wanted it back.

"Look, turn me into a toad or whatever, but I need that sword back!"

"Then go get it!" she cried.

Elph clenched his fists and growled, but the fairy snickered and rolled her eyes. She unfolded her arms and pointed at the pool.

"It's in there, you moronic baby," she snapped.

"I'm not a baby!" cried Elph.

He made to step into the pond. The second his feet touched it, he slid and fell onto his back.

The fairy laughed in pitches as high as birdsong.

"It's frozen!" he wheezed, staring up at the sky, the wind knocked from him.

"No, stupid," mocked the fairy. "You're a human. It's a fairy pool. You can't just go into a fairy pool. It'll freeze up on you. Don't they teach you kids anything these days?"

Elph's eyes stung as he pushed himself up. The fairy laughed and laughed, her hands on her hips, her antennae dancing. Her skirts twirled and her wings pumped. She laughed so hard, in fact, that she also fell onto her backside.

"Oh!" she cried.

Elph sniffed. "Serves you right. I want my sword back!"

"Maybe you should have thought of that before you threw it!" countered the fairy.

"Get it for me!" Elph roared.

The fairy stood again, dusted her off, and rounded on him. "You're the one that threw the sword. You threw it, and it landed in the pool. *I* don't have it. It's the pool's now."

Elph sagged. He really would get in trouble now.

"What will I tell Mum?" he whispered.

The fairy squinted at him. "So you didn't mean to throw it at me?" she asked.

Elph stared at her. "Why would I throw a sword at someone? It was an accident."

"Oh." She smoothed her shimmery, peacock-hued skirts. "I guess I'm so used to being punished that I—I just assumed..."

Elph raised his eyebrows. "Punished? For what?"

She shook her head and pressed her lips together.

Then he burst out, "I'm Elph."

She wriggled her nose at him. "You don't look like any elf I've ever seen. You're the most human-looking boy ever."

"Thanks, I guess," Elph laughed then. "But that's my name: Elph."

She tossed her golden-green hair, setting it flying upward. "I'm Vee."

"That's a dull name for a fairy," Elph noted.

Vee's face shone bright gold and she hissed, "That's the short version, you carrot-boy! No human could ever say my full name!"

Elph blushed and Vee glowed, and they both glared at each other.

"Anyway," said Vee, lifting her chin, "I can get your rustic little fighting twig or whatever. On one condition."

Elph shoved his hands in his pockets again and whistled. "What's that?" He dreaded the answer.

"I get the sword, and you get me out of here," replied Vee.

"Okay..." Elph crinkled his brow. "Is this some kind of trick?"

Vee snorted. "I'm a fairy. Everything I *do* is a trick."

"Well, at least you're honest about it."

"To a fault; I don't lie enough for my kind. I'm considered a rebel fairy. So here I am by this little pool, when I should be out by the sea, skimming the waves."

"What, are you some kind of sea fairy?" Come to think of it, she *did* look like she belonged not in this oak thicket but alongside seafoam and kelp.

"I'm a half sea, half sylvan fairy," Vee replied, and her expression confused Elph, but by and large he thought it was probably a form of wincing.

"Well, that's okay. The best of both worlds. I love both the sea and the woods. You're really lucky!"

Vee's face went bright, but not in the golden spectrum; it shone like the sunbeam had earlier, pure and soft.

"I never thought of it that way."

"Well, now you have," Elph grinned. "So what's the trick?"

Vee sighed and twisted her delicate fingers together. Their fingernails were deep teal green, Elph noticed. Her eyes were clear green-gold, and she blinked nervously.

"I was told that I could leave this place only through the purest word," she told him.

Elph twisted his eyebrows. "What word is that?"

"Well, if I knew that, I wouldn't be stuck, now, would I?" she cried.

"Look," said Elph, taking his hands out of his pockets and holding them out. "If you'll get me my sword, I'll help you. I promise."

Vee looked suspiciously at him. "Fine," she said. "But don't pull any human tricks with me. No telling everyone you saw me. Then I'll *really* be punished. Worse than the time I sipped coffee."

Elph snickered. "You had coffee? I thought fairies drank, like, dewdrops and things like that."

"Silly boy," Vee chided. "We're not *that* simple. I happen to enjoy coffee. It makes me glow brighter. But it does make my wings tremble."

They grinned at each other then.

She stepped forward, and her bare feet with their teal toenails stepped easily into the little vernal pool. For a second, it grew opaque, and Elph feared it had frozen. But it remained liquid, just a cloudy pale green. Vee reached down, her skirts skimming the surface, and pulled something from the shallow depths. She held it up, and the sun caught its tip.

"My sword!" Elph cried.

Vee walked out of the pool, and it instantly turned clear again. She shook off the water and then she handed the sword to Elph. He took it, and then looked quickly up at her eyes in surprise.

"It's...it's stone now!" he whispered.

"It's petrified wood," Vee corrected him.

"How..."

"Never mind," Vee replied. "You wouldn't understand."

Elph ran his hands over the hard, marbled surface of his short sword.

"Just don't go throwing it at any fairies again," Vee warned him with a lopsided grin. "You'll likely get a very different response."

Elph set the sword reverently on the ground beside him and held out his hand.

"Vee," he said shyly, blinking his ginger eyelashes and blushing, "will you be my friend?"

Vee took his hand, and instantly she sparkled all over in green, blue, gold, and other hues for which Elph had no name. She laughed in a voice like dawn and birds and crashing waves.

"You did it!" she cried. "You've freed me!"

She stretched her wings and they extended broadly. Her hair sparkled.

"How?" asked Elph, bewildered.

"That was the word," Vee told him. "'Friend'—and the answer is yes."

She smelled of the sea and lavender and new green leaves, and she pulsed her wings and rose and out of sight of him, laughing all the way. Elph picked up his sword and held it close to his chest and smiled and began his trek home.

TOO LATE FOR BERRIES

ASTRID FARALLON WAS IN big trouble. She ran as fast as she could, pumping her purple-stained legs and rubbing the marionberry juice on her hands onto her skirt. She had fallen asleep in a berry patch and awakened possibly in fairyland. She was not sure: in some ways she wished it were true, and that perhaps she might be deposited as a changeling somewhere, thereby avoiding the stern eye of her grandmother.

Her grandmother would be perched at her bay window, surveying the cobbled streets for business that was not her own: she would cluck at the Pillingtons on their afternoon stroll, dressed in too much tweed for the season; or she would sniff at the newsboy Daryl, whistling like a little train, hurtling the evening paper with so much fervor that the window box geraniums cringed from fear of receiving one of the rolled missiles amongst their cheerful petals. But chiefly, Granny would be on the lookout for *her*, and whatever she had found in forest or field.

And today, Astrid would not appear.

It was all well and good that she had anticipated being *late*, at least. She was a procrastinator. Granny knew this about her granddaughter, of course: "She was late-born and late in life in all things; late to walk, late to talk, late even to tarry, somehow, by the wayside," she had told her grandfather some years ago. He had been indulgent of Astrid's quirks, but Granny had passed more judgment both at Astrid and her grandfather (she would look over her horn-rimmed glasses at her husband with half-lidded hazel eyes in disapproval at his flippant acceptance); who knew what fate might befall such a late bloomer and daydreamer such as Astrid?

Astrid hoped that whatever situation she had found herself in, Granny would not find cause for alarm...yet. The girl looked all about her. She knew she was lost because this path did not look like any other path she had ever been on. And she could no longer hear the sea.

Oh, but the marionberry patch had been exquisite! The berries were at their most embarrassing ripeness, the sort of berries to make the market sellers disbelieve they were wild. But Astrid knew just where to look. She had climbed the great golden hill with its low scrub oaks bent from the sea breeze, and woven down through the little dales among that hill. On one side, she could see the cobalt ocean, brisk, white-capped, its horizon a fuzz and never a clear line, for the fog would soon roll in for the night, ungently: a rush and a surge. It was a creature, not a weather phenomenon; of that, she was sure. She shivered whenever she thought that, but it was a good shiver: the kind of shiver one gets when reading a juicy story. On the other side of the hill, she could see the great aquamarine-hued bay, and schooners plying it to reach the towns on the other side. Rolling gilded hills beyond number stretched off to the east, and far away the snowy peaks of the Icehall Range poked through the distortion of the summer horizon.

She had breathed in the afternoon air, redolent with herbs: sage and wild fennel, thriving in a microclimate that faced east. The darting birds and intoxicated bees circuited her quarry: a thicket of marionberries long abandoned from an old homestead. She had found it last summer, and she had never told a soul where it was. Granny had not minded that lack of data. All she cared about was a good harvest of something to trade at the market, with the bruised fruit used for canning. She never saved the good berries.

But today there had been a bit of a situation. Astrid had seen a bear! And not just any bear, but a golden bear, a quite small one. Still: it was a bear, and Astrid had not been prepared to see such a creature on her favorite hill, for there had never been talk of any bears in the area. They all lived in the preposterously tall forests to the north, across the strait. And none resembled this one. At first, she had thought it was a dog, for it chuffed and huffed and snorted and cavorted, but there was no tail on the beast, and its paws were immense. No; it was a bear, and it wanted those berries.

She had already plucked as many berries as she could and put them in her berry basket. It had two straps on it, so she could wear it like a backpack when she began the hike back to Granny's. But when the golden bear lunged toward her berry patch, she shrieked, startling the bear, which stood on its hind legs for a moment in confusion and looked all around itself. Then it huffed again, but Astrid could swear it was a huff of disbelief as if it didn't know where it was. At any rate, Astrid did not wait to find out what would happen next. She ran, and then she fell. Out spilled the berries, and she landed on them and scraped her knees besides. She did not hesitate long to lament the loss of her harvest, and she got up and ran again, and then she found herself here, in a dark wood, with deep teal branches stretching over her on either side.

Pine needles carpeted the path beneath her feet. She shuffled through them. Astrid knew it was fairyland. One doesn't just run from a golden bear on a hill and end up in a forest within seconds. She looked behind her. The bear had not followed. She sniffed: something rich and fragrant met her nose, and she decided to follow the scent on the trail before her, which led through a tunnel of trees. She was completely alone, yet she thought she heard music.

"No," she said to herself firmly. "They always play music. I should not follow the music. But it smells good, and I am hungry. This is how kids are eaten. Lured in by music and food. It works every time, and I'm to be someone's dinner, I just know it!"

Still, in this conversation with herself, she managed to dread returning to Granny empty-handed. And very late. For in these woods it was twilight, as if time had rolled forward.

"Maybe it would be better if I *were* eaten," she mumbled, thinking of Granny's stern gaze through her glasses like a disapproving owl. She knew Granny would give her extra chores. But really, Astrid did not mean to be late. It's just how she was.

She heard laughter. She stopped walking. She turned her head, and she gasped.

To her left there sat a little house tucked back in the trees in a small clearing. She nodded to herself, confident in her arrival in fairyland. Houses did not just appear suddenly in the woods. Usually. Or so she thought.

A little coil of blue smoke rose from the chimney of the house, up through the small cylinder of treeless space above it, and into the sky. The smells of cooking made Astrid's stomach growl.

"I'm absolutely going to be eaten," she moaned, "but maybe they'll fill me up first. It might be worth it! I'm so hungry."

The laugh rang out again, and then a door opened, and a rectangle of silver-gold light shone from it. A figure stood in shadow there: tall, willowy, with hair swirling around the knees.

"Astrid Garnet Farallon!" called the figure in a clear, low woman's voice. "Come in, come in! Dinner awaits!"

Astrid self-consciously looked down at her stained and scratched legs.

"I'm really gross and dirty, ma'am," she called back. "And you might eat me. But I would be stringy! You wouldn't like that."

The lady's laughter echoed in the little clearing, and Astrid found herself walking closer. The house had little teal gables carved like ocean waves, with flowers painted on them...strange flowers she had never seen before, but had heard about in stories from seafarers who had made it to the tropical isles and back again, somehow. Now *that* was real magic, she thought. Just like this, but different.

Even as she approached the lady in the house, Astrid asked, "How did you know my middle name?"

"How could I not?" the lady replied, and Astrid did not know how to respond to that.

The lady turned so that Astrid could see her profile, and she was quite tall and sharp-featured, but with an elegant, smooth, long neck, adorned by no jewelry. She wore a dress that seemed to shift between palest purple, pink, and green, like auroras from the north (Astrid had heard tales of them as well). About the lady's waist, a vivid purple ribbon hung as a belt, and a small conch shell was hooked on it. That was the woman's only adornment. Her hair flickered and flowed, a deep golden brown, all the way past her knees, sleek yet wild at the same time.

"I am Myriad," she announced. "Do come inside."

"To be eaten?" Astrid asked, and she looked Myriad straight in her strange dark eyes, their color uncertain to the girl.

"To eat, dear Astrid," Myriad replied, smiling.

Inside there burned a hearth fire, and a round table stood set for two. In the center of the table, a short violet vase of flowers drew Astrid's eye; the flowers were tropical, like those painted on the gable. Astrid turned her head a moment to look at the rest of the small house, and found it most cozy, and could see more of the vivid, redolent flowers tucked among comfortable-looking chairs. The rug in the living room was woven so that it looked like one large blossom. Astrid turned back to the table and was startled to see it laden with all manner of foods, yet Myriad had not left her side, and no one else could be seen in the small house.

"Do—do you have a helper?" the girl asked.

"Not at the moment," Myriad replied, gesturing for Astrid to sit. The girl did so and watched as the lady sat across from her. "Unfortunately, my helper has gone missing."

"Oh," said Astrid, snatching four small sandwiches from a little tower of plates in front of her. Then, between chews, "I'm sorry to hear that."

Myriad smiled and sipped from her amber-hued wine. Astrid drank water, but it was not like the water her Granny served. This was biting cold and vibrant and seemed to dance its path from her lips to her stomach.

"I thought perhaps you might have seen my assistant. His name is Jeremy, and he is a golden bear."

Astrid nearly spat out her water. She coughed.

"The bear! The bear in the berry patch!" she cried.

Myriad laughed, her hair coiling all around her as she sat until it rested curled about her waist. "Is that what drew him away? Oh, Jeremy. I did warn him not to. For that is likely what led you to me."

Astrid slyly reached for a scone with one hand and a sandwich with the other.

"What do you mean?" she asked.

Myriad set her wine down and folded her fingers together. Astrid realized the lady had no food on her plate, and that made the girl uneasy. Myriad saw her worried look, however, and began to take some of the food and eat it herself. Astrid let out a sigh of relief and ate some fruit next.

"Whenever Jeremy ventures into your land, someone else ends up here in return," Myriad explained. "It's a bit of a problem, but fortunately my dear bear does not do this often. I think the smell of your berries drew him this time. Even I could smell them. But Jeremy is a bear! So, his nose is keener than mine."

A clock chimed behind them, and Astrid jumped.

"Where are we? And what time is it?" she asked. "I'm so late. I'm going to be in heaps of trouble. I even lost some of the berries, running from the bear—I mean Jeremy. I'm not used to seeing bears there!"

Myriad laughed again. "No, I would imagine not; not there. And to answer your question, you are simply here, in my home, in the forest. Not far from your home in terms of distance, but perhaps in other ways," and Myriad peeked over her shoulder at the clock, its pendulum waving slowly back and forth.

Astrid considered the lady's words. "Time?" she asked. Myriad took a sip of wine and smiled mysteriously.

"We should get you home soon," the lady said, "and see about Jeremy's return. You'll have to do this at the same time. Finish your food and I will guide you back."

Astrid did so, and she glanced wistfully inside the delicious nook of a home. She could see framed pictures out of the corner of her eyes, but when she turned to look at them there was nothing there but soft stucco walls. She sighed. She did not really want to go but knew Granny would not only disapprove of her being late, but also might be worried by now as well.

Myriad led her outside of the house, and then she took the shell from the belt at her waist and touched it to the doorknob. Astrid heard a little click.

"A key?" she asked.

"After a fashion," answered Myriad, a smirk curling on her lips. "Follow me, dear Astrid."

Myriad led her into the forest and came upon a path. It was far more open and well-lit than the one Astrid had emerged from earlier. Looking up, the girl could see a sky clustered with brilliant stars. She lifted her finger and traced shapes in those stars...and found them unfamiliar.

Myriad reached for her other hand and pulled her gently along, and the woman's hair rippled behind her as they walked.

"Do you smell it?" Myriad asked suddenly.

"Smell what?" Astrid asked. All that she could see ahead was a long, dim lane under great trees. All that she could smell was...and she gasped.

"The sea!" she exclaimed.

"Yes," said Myriad, smiling. "And here we must part, dear child."

Astrid squeezed Myriad's hand. "You're so nice. Can I come back?"

Myriad tilted her head down and said, "I am not sure. I do not think you will find yourself lost again."

Astrid thought about that and bit her lip. She really would have loved to come back here at any time. *At any time*, she thought suddenly. And she felt Myriad's hand slip out of hers. She heard a chuffing sound, and the air in front of her wavered, and a golden bear rushed toward her. She cried out and swerved, and in a brief second, she closed her eyes cried out, "Jeremy!"

She opened her eyes to see the bear, but then she had to squint. She was in the brilliant afternoon sunlight, and she blinked. She smelled wild fennel and the tang of the ocean.

"Oh," she said, a bit sad, "I'm back."

For she stood again on the headland between ocean and bay. She walked all around the spot where she had been earlier, and everything lay still. There was no bear. Even the bees had gone home. Her basket lay on the ground, and she walked over and bent down to pick it up.

"Granny will be so disappointed I spilled the berries," she muttered, "and now it really is too late to pick more."

But she found the basket quite heavy. She opened it and gasped. For the basket was filled completely with berries, unblemished, plump, dark, and glistening. And laid gently over their top a gossamer handkerchief rested, in shifting aurora colors, with the letter "A" embroidered on it by a skilled hand.

"Thank you, Myriad! And thank you, Jeremy!" she said aloud, but no one was there to answer her.

She began her hike down to her Granny's home and noted that even her legs looked clean; gone were the stains of earlier. She walked slowly on the cobblestone street, thinking back to the lovely home of Myriad and Jeremy, and wondered if she might ever see them again. Then she looked up, for she almost collided with a boy. It was Daryl, the newsboy. He tipped his dark brown beret at her and winked with his dark brown eyes, whistled, and moved on. She watched him launch papers along his route, and then she turned to look at the bay window where her grandmother sat, watching her. Astrid chewed her lip.

She walked forward, climbed the steps to Granny's home, and entered the sitting room, where Granny turned to look up at her.

"Well!" said Granny, a tiny smile forming on her lips, her glasses reflecting a lit lantern on a table in front of the window. "For once, you're not late!"

"What?" said Astrid, truly surprised. "I thought I was very late! I—" and she stopped. She did not know what to say. "I—I found some nice berries."

Granny peered into Astrid's open basket and clapped her hands together.

"Marvelous!" she said to the girl. "Now let's have some of these for tea."

"I can't believe I'm not late!" Astrid said, and she surreptitiously tucked the new handkerchief into her skirt pocket. Granny grinned.

"You're just in time," she said.

A BREAK FOR PASTRIES

NEPENTHE PECK SAT NEXT to her screened window, which looked out at the distant golden hill and the giant ancient tower that Myra said looked made of peppermint. It *was* red and white, and Myra's keen beak wanted very much to tap into the giant thing and taste it for herself. Her person, Nepenthe, would not allow this, of course.

Myra was a Pacific parrotlet, a green slip of a bird, a feisty emerald comma with wings that liked to break up Nepenthe's monotony. Just now she spied with her tiny brown eyes a trundling little cart in the Skillet, the round park just beyond the eucalyptus and scrub oak.

She leaned over and stretched her little neck out, turned her head over her shoulder, and peeped, "Look!"

"What is it, Myra?" asked Nepenthe, her mind lost in a plot that she could not quite untangle.

"It's the baker!" chirped Myra. She tilted her head, then flew over to her person's shoulder and began nibbling her chin. "You've tapped your chin with the cap off again," the wee bird noted, poking Nepenthe's ink-stained chin with her beak.

"Easy!" said Nepenthe, and Myra clucked and burrowed under the dark auburn waves of hair and began pulling them methodically through her beak, grooming as if they were her own bright feathers.

"Are you going down, then?" asked Myra, stopping her grooming of Nepenthe long enough to draw her own tiny feathers through her beak, and then she rubbed that beak on the gland above her tail and set back to sleeking the feathers.

"Oh, I don't know," sighed Nepenthe. "I'm stuck on this one passage, you see."

"I don't see," tutted Myra, and she emerged from the tunnel of Nepenthe's hair to meet the young woman's eye. "I want berry crumble. I want muffins. I want croissants."

"Myra," laughed Nepenthe, "those are bigger than you are!"

Myra fluffed her feathers and shrugged. "When did that ever stop me? Or you, for that matter." She tapped her beak on Nepenthe's chin again. "Go get something! I'm starving."

Nepenthe held her forefinger out for Myra to step up. She carried the little bird to her cage, outfitted inside and out with all manner of toys, real wood branches, and no shortage of both fresh and pelleted food.

"You definitely live up to our last name, cheeky," said Nepenthe, and she kissed Myra on the beak and placed her inside the cage. Myra promptly flitted down to her water dish and began splashing and dunking in it, flinging drops everywhere. Nepenthe smirked indulgently and stretched. She glanced back at her notebook. "I suppose I needed a break," she confessed.

Myra sprayed water out and tilted her wet head back to say, "You do! And it's a good thing you have me to remind you."

"I suppose that's true," mused Nepenthe. She bound her hair into a low bun at the base of her neck and donned a vest. The fog began to crest the hill, to envelop Myra's huge peppermint tower. It was early November, and despite the relatively balmy weather, an underlying nip in the air bit at the neck and waist lately.

Nepenthe locked her door and walked down the carpeted old stairs, her hands running along the bumps of decades of paint layers. The carpet was ancient wine-hued paisley, and the stairs protested any footfalls. She heard familiar scratches inside room 14, and that door opened just long enough for a little white dog to walk out and face her.

"Bakery?" he asked, his shining little button-black eyes beseeching her.

Nepenthe sighed. "Really, Roger?" she asked the little dog. "I'm not so sure Mel would want you to—"

She heard three short coughs and a high voice call, "Bring me two of the apple chaussons! I'll pay ye when ye get back!"

"All right, Mel," called Nepenthe. She turned back to Roger, who dipped his head down in a play bow.

"Can you guess what I want?" he asked, with his little silky white tail wagging.

"I am pretty sure I can," said Nepenthe with a nod.

Roger trotted back into his apartment and closed the door with his left paw. She heard Mel call him over and admonish him for being so forward, but she did so gently.

Now it was time for Nepenthe to dart down and out of the building before any *more* doors opened. For it was no secret that she was generous if asked; she would get pastries for anyone, but she often did not help herself.

She made it outside, past the waddling bus that chuffed and sighed at the bus stop, yawning out its passengers, who looked every bit as sleepy as it did; it soon fell to dozing until the driver tapped the horn. Then it snorted with high dudgeon, closed its doors, and shuffled down the street.

Nepenthe skirted the Great Horseshoe Park, with its conservatory, walking paths, and secretive woods where the city's wild foxes liked to gossip over tea, and she found the walkway to take her back to the Skillet Park the next block over. Oftentimes, from her window, she would watch the comings and goings of people and animals of all sorts, and many would stop and chat, their wind-caught words drifting in broken bits up to her window where she wrote. Sometimes, parts of their conversations made it into her writing.

Today she was in the thick of it herself, and she found her destination: the bakery cart of Mister Fluffen and Quibblestone, the baker duo of much renown in these parts. Mister Fluffen was a grizzled old chap, possibly a man, but perhaps a tree, and depending on the day, maybe even both. He would plant himself and his cart in the earth of Skillet Park when families with young children came to play there, and Quibblestone, the copper-hued Vizsla, stood on his hind legs to help serve customers.

On this day, Quibblestone sniffed her from afar and said, "I take it Roger wants a treat for tea?"

"How'd you guess?" Nepenthe responded dryly.

"How's the old chap, anyway?" asked Quibblestone, and looking sideways to see that no children were about, he dropped to all fours and snatched a bag of bone biscuits and delivered them to Nepenthe before she even made it to the cart.

"Ah, you know Roger," said Nepenthe, and she gave Quibblestone a bag of coins. "Attentive as ever. Mel wants some of the apple chaussons, by the way. I've enough money in there for those too."

"I don't even count yours," Quibblestone told her quietly. "Your money's no good here, as they say."

"Oh, Quibblestone," whispered Nepenthe, and the two of them glanced at Mister Fluffen. He stood propped against his cart, railroad cap slipping down over his eyes, his hands over his round belly, and he snored.

"What'll it be, then?" asked the dog quietly.

Nepenthe put her hands on her hips and pondered. Quibblestone then quickly stood on all his hind legs and walked that way back to the cart. She watched him don an apron and prepare for two young children who spied him from the playground swings and shouted. He looked at Nepenthe with a pained expression.

"You might want to hurry," he called. "When there's two, there'll be twenty, you know."

So, Nepenthe approached the cart, and its faded red paint matched the faded red trousers of Mister Fluffen, who still stood snoring. But as soon as she had made it to the cart and admired its little open shelves of glistening pastries and seeded breads, the fellow gave a loud snort and straightened his cap.

"Well, if it isn't our Nepenthe!" he cried, as if he hadn't been sleeping the past several minutes. He extended a ruddy hand, and she took it and shook it; it felt like smooth tree bark.

"Hello, Mister Fluffen!" she answered, and she brought forth another bag of coins, even though she did not need to. "I'll take a muffin, a croissant, and one of those berry tarts, please."

"Little Myra's hungry then, eh?" asked Mister Fluffen with a chuckle. As Quibblestone dealt with the children, Mister Fluffen scooped up Nepenthe's order and placed them inside a striped paper bag. He tossed in a peppermint stick. He lowered his eyes and grinned at Nepenthe. "I know I shouldn't, but she'll enjoy gnawing on it," he said.

Nepenthe suppressed a sigh and nodded. "Thank you! And now I'm off." She waved at Quibblestone, who called over, "Hi to Roger, then!"

And off she wandered under the low-bent, swaying trees in the fading, creamy light, back to the sidewalk and around the building to her apartment. The Great Horseshoe Park's dark cypresses and redwoods allowed just a bit of the setting sun to send a shaft through them and set her hair ablaze, which made her self-conscious. She looked up to see Roger's little face against his apartment's window, and then he dropped out of sight.

She ambled back into the apartment, up the four flights of old stairs, and Roger met her in the hallway.

"Well?" he asked, stepping on his short legs over to her quickly.

Nepenthe knelt and gave him one of the special biscuits.

"Hand-selected by Quibblestone himself," she assured Roger.

He nodded at her, and she could swear that he winked.

"Wait," she said suddenly, "how special are these biscuits?"

Roger sneezed and said, "Never you mind, thank you! But tell me, how's the old fellow doing? You know, he was quite the award winner back in the day."

"Quibblestone?" Nepenthe gasped in disbelief. "Well, that explains why he's so nimble on his feet, I suppose. He's doing well. He braced for the children."

Roger laugh-barked. She handed him the bag with the rest of the biscuits and the bag with Mel's apple chaussons.

"Thank ye, honey!" yelled Mel from somewhere in the recesses of the apartment.

"Many thanks, Nepenthe. All my best to Myra!" said Roger, and he picked up both bags gingerly with his bright little teeth, entered his home, and shut the door with his right paw.

Off the pair were, arguing and discussing, and Nepenthe heard the rustling of the bags as they enjoyed their treasures. She began walking up the ancient stairs, and she heard a distant loud *clang*.

"Ah, the fog has blown in," she mused aloud. She would have to go and shut the roof door, for it had blown open again.

She turned the old crystal doorknob and entered just as the sun had finally set. Myra yawned in her cage as Nepenthe turned on the lights. She opened the cage, and Myra flew to her shoulder. The two sat at the little table off the kitchen; Myra jumped down to the table itself, directly next to the pastries. Nepenthe spread the baked treasures onto a plate and let Myra pick and choose whatever she wanted. The little emerald bird peeped and clucked, and her eyes glazed over in contentment. Nepenthe's eyes wandered back to her notebook. Myra nudged her hand with her beak.

"Not yet!" chided the little bird. "Feed yourself before you feed the world with your words."

Nepenthe laughed. "Good advice, dear Myra."

THE STORY LIGHT

TISH BEGGED HER GRANDMOTHER for one more story.

Grandma chuckled. "I'll tell you about the Story Light."

"What's the Story Light?" Tish asked.

Grandma folded her crinkly hands. She began, "When I was little, my family lived far from a library. I wanted to read more than anything. I wanted adventures.

"Late one day, an old man with a tall hat drove a pickup truck out to the farm my parents worked. My parents went to meet him."

Grandma hugged Tish's shoulders.

"This man called himself Professor G. He said, 'I've got a big stack of adventures to give you! But you must work my Story Light.' My brothers and I looked at Mother and Dad. They winked.

"He held a strange lantern in his hands, faceted on all sides. He said, 'If you can work the Story Light, you can have every adventure.' 'How?' we asked.

"Professor G held it up. 'All you have to do is believe in stories. Can you do that?' 'Yes!' we all hollered. 'I believe in stories, I believe in stories!' I shouted.

"And look at that! The funny lantern hovered and glowed, casting light on his books. 'I knew you could!' he said. 'If you believe in stories, and read and share them, you can make a brilliant light.'"

"What happened to him?" Tish asked.

Grandma beamed at her. "Professor G wrote his own stories. They named a library after him. And best of all? The library looks just like his Story Light."

FALLING UPWARD INTO STARLIGHT

RADIADNE TRIED TO LET go and allow the warm updraft to carry her upward, but her wings instinctively pulsed in panic. She closed her pewter eyes, feeling the familiar dizziness of anxiety spin through her. She swallowed.

Pelter watched through slitted, teal eyes, their eyelids bronze bespeckled with green, and clucked their tongue. Pelter had coached Radiadne through her tense nerves many times, but today was a crucial test for all fairies of age. The sapphire cliffs of the land of Drillenwe provided the final flight exam to graduate with a master's in updraft gliding. The problem was, Radiadne could not glide; she could only flail, and spring skittishly back to the cliff.

"You'll never get a family this way, Radiadne," her mother had cautioned during her last failed attempt. "Look at your sister: three fine grandchildren she's given me! What you'll be, goodness knows."

Radiadne had sighed. She and Pelter enjoyed their quiet relationship. Pelter was a golden fairy with green wings, and she was lavender with fire-hued wings. Neither needed any traditional validation for their future; they simply *were*.

"You're thinking about your mom again." Pelter clucked again. "Just. Breathe. It's fine to feel dizzy; breathe through it, and you won't panic. Breathe through it. I'll join you."

So Radiadne stood at the edge of the sapphire cliffs and stared at Pelter. Pelter breathed in through their nose and out through their mouth, slowly and deeply.

"I don't need the destiny anyone else imagines for me," whispered Radiadne. Pelter grinned and nodded, teal eyes shining. Radiadne pumped her wings, then flew backward, as if floating on water. The updraft caught her, and she sailed skyward, smiling. Pelter soon glided alongside her, just as the first stars shone through the violet and indigo twilight.

A SWIRL OF LEAVES AND SAND

IF HE HELD HIS fingers just right, Seth could see the sun glow through his flesh. But now the sun weakened as September waned, and the bustle of the bayfront dwindled as the last of summer's tourists nabbed their trinkets and headed back to parts unknown, but likely to work and to school. Such was the way of Septembers at Cape Slattery: the sea sighed, and the winds lowed, the sands shifted, and the world pivoted ahead of the equinox and the winding down of the year.

Seth's parents lived upstate in verdant Arlendale, surrounded by green mountains now tinged with amber and crimson and tawny brown. He preferred the shore. Autumn unfolded more slowly, unless one of the decaying tropical systems churned its way up the coast and parked itself before the cold waters of the north Atlantic siphoned its vigor. Then there were the winds.

It happened: the storm dissipated, the tourists having watched with interest but not alarm, the lifeguards frantic, barking warnings against the undertow and rip tides. It had never come ashore, but the winds asserted themselves. The dance of bamboo and metal windchimes and the occasional stronger gusts jolted him awake. He rose feeling disgruntled by it all and resenting the tourists. This was *his* beach. He was a painter, and while tourists adored his vivid depictions of the summer shore as bespoke memories caught in acrylic, he preferred when they had gone, and he would set his easel upon the end of the boardwalk and capture the smears of late afternoon pastels tinged with gold.

But not today.

He carried his easel in a strap over his shoulder. He grabbed a coffee and closed his eyes to the first sharp tang as it scorched its way down his throat. He tipped the barista, who would soon return to college. In two weeks, this shore would house only the wind and the sand, the shops closing until the next year, the town given over to its longer fishing roots, before tourism exacted a price upon the shore.

Yet he would miss it, and he resented himself for that. The truth was, he was listless and bored, and the absence of the tourists troubled him, for he faced a morosity of spirit and loneliness as the sun angle dipped. And he would lose his precious light.

He propped the easel up. He looked through his fingers at the sun. A toddler clipped his thigh while her frantic father stammered an apology and raced after her. She dropped a too-early ice cream and it sat, cone skyward, upon the boardwalk's end, where developers had reluctantly surrendered to the adjacent national seashore. There, the father now plucked the daughter from the beach-grass throttled dunes. Her high-pitched squeals made Seth chuckle. He understood.

Sometimes, after the crowds had gone, he'd sprinted off into the wilder parts of the beach alone. There was something about them. Set back from the shore, a thicket of woods creaked and swayed, and so it was today. The father-daughter pair returned to civilization, making their way toward primary-colored beach shovels and rainbow whirligigs and stuffed bears with little shirts that said "Cape Slattery." Selecting one of those, the girl was satisfied, her ice cream forgotten. Seth smiled to himself and then sighed.

After that bit of excitement, the wind made its presence known. The woods shivered and rustled and whispered, gossiping about...something. He raised his eyes to them, and just as he did, a strong gust toppled his easel, sending his canvas spinning like a heavy kite into the air. Spouting an epithet, he bounded after it, and yet it eluded him, and the wind saw fit to cast it into the sea.

He stared, open-mouthed, at the white froth and the dark grey green expanse with its many whitecaps.

A whispering sound rushed in his ears, and a voice said, "No painting for you today."

He spun around and saw no one. At first.

But by and by some of the leaves from the woods swirled onto the beach and intermixed with a small vortex of sand, and there Seth beheld...someone. He blinked, took off his glasses, rubbed them with his shirt, placed them back on his face, and looked again. And there she was: a woman made of leaf and sand and light, her hair long dark green ribbons like floating kelp, her raiment mother-of-pearl and long grasses encircled by a belt of sand dollars. She gazed at him, and he felt as though one of the cold waves had crashed over him, for there was no warmth there in her sea eyes, no smile upon her seafoam-green face.

"What are you?" he managed to whisper.

Then came a smirk, and a smile like sun upon the wavetops after a dark cloud breaks.

"I am of the in between," she answered. Her form shifted and rippled like sunlight through trees. "I am the woods and the shore and the moment between summer and autumn."

"Are you the only one?"

He gaped in awe, and wished he'd brought one of those little disposable cameras for sale at the boardwalk. He glanced behind him and saw then that there was no boardwalk: indeed, there was nothing but sea and sand and kittiwakes and sandpipers and woods, as far as he could see. Only the moan of the shore; no staccato wind chimes.

"Where am I?" he asked.

"You are where you are," she replied.

"Where is everything *else*?"

"It is there, but that is not important. Listen."

Seth blinked. "Okay. I'm listening."

"No, listen," she insisted, and she raised her hands and her head aloft. So Seth listened: to the sea, to the wind, to the birds, to the leaves.

"I hear them," he murmured.

"They are always here," she told him. "You will never be alone."

Seth said, "Oh!" and she smiled at him again, and then she dissipated, a swirl of leaves and sand, and nothing more.

IN THE WOOD OF FROST AND SHADOW

ROSE AND PEWTER SKIES heralded the early dusk upon the land of Opaldalen, and a new layer of powdered snow lay in soft tufts among the hillocks and valleys. A little red-capped tomte, Rödhatt, made his afternoon rounds, slipping among the opalescent shadows about the farms as their human denizens settled in for the longest night.

"What news on the shortest day, my friends?" Rödhatt asked the sheep in one of the barns.

"We have been fed well for the Solstice, tomte Rödhatt!" spoke the ewe, Tistel. She lay among fresh straw, strewn earlier by the farmer.

Rödhatt nodded approvingly. "Even so, I have some nice oats for you," he clucked, and he brought forth some of the grains from the little pouch about his waist.

"Ah, thank you, Rödhatt," murmured Tistel, and she and her fellow ewes munched pleasantly.

Rödhatt climbed into the hayloft and found the family of honey-furred mice waking from their slumber.

"It is a bit early for you, is it not?" he teased as the weanlings stretched and ventured forth, bouncing about like so much popcorn popping, their frisky tails flailing about.

"Ah, but they are young," said their mother, a lovely, amber-colored mouse named Klöver, who blinked from fatigue.

Rödhatt pulled at his white beard and adjusted his red cap, and said, "Dear Klöver, the trials of the early days of motherhood seem tiring indeed! Tuck a bit of this away." He handed her little kernels made of crushed pine nuts and honey. She flicked her tail at him in thanks, and he carried on.

High in the eaves of the barn, Rödhatt spied a pair of redpolls, quite fluffed up, huddling for warmth. They looked down at him under ruddy and grey feathers but made no sound.

"I do think you will enjoy the seed balls as well, friends," he called up, and Mister Redpoll flitted down to greet him, dipped into a grateful bow, pushed seed balls into his mouth, and leapt back up to Missus Redpoll.

"Happy Solstice, dear friends!" Rödhatt called to the remaining animals, and he carried on his way.

The sky became the watercolor wash of the brief day of the north, a twilight from which the sun would not return just yet: purple and teal and indigo, and the first pinpricks of stars shone forth. Rödhatt could see the candles in the windows of the farm, and he passed just underneath one, the top of his scarlet hat almost reaching the window frame. He found a pail among the heaps of snow and set it upside down so that he might climb upon it. He did so, and he kept his white whiskers and bright red nose out of sight while he gazed in upon the scene.

There were three children, their cheeks scarlet from laughter and song, and from the crackling woodstove off in one corner, creamy white and painted with scrolls of blue flowers from floor to ceiling. The golden floors were swept, the lanterns brightly polished, and garlands of evergreen boughs and little wooden dala horses decorated the festive space. Rödhatt smelled cardamom and cinnamon and, turning his head just a bit, beheld the children's mother, her hair braided into a bun at her neck, her white apron coated in spices, her hands white with flour. She rolled cookie dough, and the children dashed forward to cut stars and hearts from it, snicking bits of the cookie dough when their mother wasn't looking. This made Rödhatt chuckle to himself.

Then one of the children said, breathless, "Might we see a tomte, Mother? Can we go and look?"

Rödhatt ducked out of sight, just in case; for while adults could not see him, a child might.

"No, darling," called their mother. "We have our Yule cookies to bake! See here, maybe you can make a tomte cookie."

The children cried out in hoots of delight and circled around their mother's skirts.

"Besides," said their mother, "you may see gifts from the tomte if you behave well; and in the morning, we can check for footprints in the snow!"

So the kitchen grew into a pleasant hive of more cookie making and baking, and the bright and cheerful songs that only children anticipating Yule could ever sing.

Rödhatt stepped down and wandered on, away from the brilliant warmth of the farmhouse, its ceiling piled high with snow now tinted periwinkle in the coming of night.

The snowbanks swooped and swirled like twilit meringue upon the land, and the pale trunks of woods behind the farmhouse stood in quiet repose as the night grew darker. The tomte wandered through those woods, and out the other side, and toward the deeper forest of tall firs. The snow was more manageable now, and his light feet no longer sank as much upon the snowdrifts, for the great dark boughs of the firs shielded the forest floor somewhat.

By and by, he sensed the eyes of something upon him, and heard an impatient shivering, and then beheld the falling of a chunk of snow from a high fir top. There stood an owl, its golden-bright eye staring down at him; it was nearly his height, he judged, but he knew that it was no enemy.

"Hello up there, friend owl," Rödhatt called, doffing his red cap for a moment and then pulling it back on.

"Hello, tomte," replied the owl, staring at him. "I do not suppose you bring me fat treasures from the eaves of yon farmer's barns, do you?" The owl clicked its sharp beak together three times, as a person might smack their lips.

Rödhatt laughed. "I am sorry, friend owl, I do not; for I take care of the little ones who need shelter."

"It is just as well," conceded the owl, preening, "but do you take care of the larger animals as well?"

"I try," Rödhatt replied.

"Then it might interest you," the owl suggested, "to look for a stag to the north, for he seems to be in a predicament."

"Does he!" exclaimed the tomte. "Well, then, you have gifted me well with this knowledge, friend owl. I will leave some kernels for you. For while they may not be made of the prey you prefer, they will sustain you on the longest night."

The owl then glided down, immense, as pale as the snow itself, its eyes hauntingly amber. Rödhatt heard the wind whistle through its wings. The tomte did not flinch, however, for he knew, as a forest spirit, he was in no way at risk from the great bird of the night. The owl scooped up the seed balls and flicked its wings gratefully before launching back up into the treetops.

On the tomte traveled, and by and by, he beheld a green cast upon the night snow. He looked up to see the aurora burst forth above him; now a dragon, then a bird, then a curtain, flickering between green and violet and stretching high, so high...high into the land of the spirits between the heavens and the earth that liked to dance on winter nights.

One of them slid down, presently, to dance above the ground before Rödhatt, and the ionosprite pirouetted in its strange way while singing in a voice that sounded rather like a song filtered through electric pops and whistles. Its shape was slender and green, an indefinable being, its crown grown from its sharp face and ending in bright purple points.

"Hello," said Rödhatt, bowing. "I see that you and your kinfolk dance to the Solstice songs this evening!"

"We do," said the ionosprite in its odd voice. "Won't you come and join us?" It pointed up, and another three aurora sprites descended before Rödhatt.

They danced in the snow, or so it first appeared; but the tomte noticed that their feet did not, in fact, actually touch the surface of the earth. He nodded to himself, for the old stories told that should they touch the earth, they would freeze to it, unable to return to their home in the ionosphere. The ionosprites dared, however, for such was their joy at the coming of the northern Solstice; exuberance arched in the sky above and the lands below. The great archer made of stars sailed slowly in the winter night sky also, and the dancing ionosprites would pause and lift their arms as if aiming arrows into the sky. They wheeled and pranced and dipped and came ever closer to the earth.

Rödhatt watched their brazen moves and could see minute details that other beings could not. And so, he knew how very close indeed the ionosprites danced to the surface: mere nanometers above it, never once touching.

Rödhatt also knew that, if he dared to join the ionosprites, he could also never return to his home upon the earth. He had heard those stories as well and knew from his many countless years that it was better to remain where you can thrive, rather than try to live somewhere inhospitable or even deadly. He knew, as well, that should the humans ever find out about the spirits of sky and forest, they would never stop looking for them. This was why so many of the spirits and fairies and animals hid whenever humans were about.

Not everything is for them, he reasoned. *But what is for them is wondrous, if only they should realize it.*

Yet on the Solstice, many of their kind did realize it, which was one reason why he enjoyed observing their celebrations. It was a moment when all appreciated the return of the light to the north, while far to the south, his austral counterparts welcomed the brightness of the Summer Solstice. But they could not see the ionosprites anymore, for they danced out of sight, warming in the summer sun.

Rödhatt watched the sprites dancing and sighed. "My friends, I must decline, although I welcome the invitation most gratefully. I wish you a lovely dance on this longest night."

"Farewell, then, tomte!" they called through buzzing voices, and they danced back up into the shimmering, coiling curtains above.

Rödhatt trudged onward, and finally, among the dark firs, he found the tracks of a great stag. Following them, he heard soft singing as frost fairies strung pale lights among the boughs of the firs, which reflected upon the snow, warm in hue but cold to the touch, as befitted frost fairies. Between the lights of the fairies and the aurora above, it was a joyful scene for Solstice. Still, the owl's news had troubled Rödhatt, and so he ventured forth.

There among a clearing, between clusters of holly bushes and deeply snow-bent trees curling over at their tops, a stag sat, exhausted. And even though the tomte was quite silent, the stag could smell him, and he struggled to get up, and snorted in frustration.

A distant howl rang through the snowy valley, followed by another, and another.

Rödhatt paused.

"My Yule stag friend," he murmured, "are you hurt?"

The stag sniffed and did not answer.

Rödhatt nodded to himself. "You are a fine stag, and proud," he said to the creature. "Yet it is yuletide, and all the beasts are hungry in the cold night. Hear the wolves in the distance?"

"Of course," grumbled the stag in a gruff voice.

"Ah, friend stag, do not let pride prevent your rescue," said the tomte warmly. "I can help ease you out."

The stag heaved a great sigh and dipped his impressive antlers.

The full moon burst forth just then, over the treetops, setting the tips of the stag's antlers sparkling, and making the snow look cast with diamonds.

"You are in full sight of everything now, friend," whispered Rödhatt. "We must not let the night pass with you in this predicament, for I fear it will go worse for you if we do not get you out soon."

So Rödhatt pulled at the tangle of logs that the stag had stumbled upon, and the stag snorted in discomfort. The logs had been covered by a snowdrift, and so the stag had missed seeing them.

"Foolishness," the stag chided himself.

"Nonsense," returned Rödhatt. "None of us can see all things all the time."

The stag gazed down at the little fellow as he removed a hoof from its lodged spot under the logs.

"Isn't that true of you, though, tomte?" asked the stag, pulling his leg out. He swung it back and forth, testing it, and he pawed at the ground, sending up sparkles of snow.

Rödhatt chuckled softly. "My friend, the legends tell of many stories about me, and only some of them are true."

The stag stood robust and strong then and bent his head down to Rödhatt. Rödhatt rubbed the fur between the stag's antlers.

"I thank you, friend tomte," said the stag.

"Rödhatt," answered the tomte.

"I thank you, friend Rödhatt," said the stag.

"I wish you safe travels, friend," said Rödhatt. "Have some of my grains before you go, and mind you stay clear of the bright moonlight. For though the people celebrate in their homes, they need not know you are afoot here."

"Indeed," said the stag gratefully, munching on the oat mixture. He then marched off, and Rödhatt watched him slip away from the moonlight and out of sight, deep into the forest. The cries of distant wolves faded also, so Rödhatt breathed a sigh of relief.

Rödhatt began his walk back through the forest, and the moon then shown so brightly that even the aurora faded a bit. Long shadows cast in ultramarine hues on the snow heaps before the tomte. He could feel the turn of the earth and sense the movement of the stars above, and he knew the moment that the humans called midnight, and he felt satisfied.

Within his pockets, he still bore seed kernels and oats, and so under the twinkling fairy lights set upon the fir trees, under the moon and the aurora, he sowed them hither and yon beneath the trees. Some of them he cast upon the open snow, for bright little eyes in the dawn of the next day to find. For he knew that not all creatures would respond to him, or slink forth from their shelters; no, not even for him.

He strode back through the forest and beheld the frost fairies once more. They had woven cold, shining lace from ice, and hung rectangles of them out for him to see.

"What do you think, dear Rödhatt?" one called to him, displaying an especially ornate ice tapestry.

Rödhatt smiled up at the fairy. "I think the children will love to see that in their windowpanes when they awaken!" he said, and the fairies bowed and curtsied in delight. They would deliver their frost art to the windows of the nearby farms, to charm everyone in the morning.

Solstice gave Rödhatt the opportunity to take stock of the comings and goings in the forest and in the fields, and to make sure that the creatures both inside and outside their shelters might survive the cold northern nights. It would not be long before the sun's return made the Solstice a distant memory. Rödhatt had seen the circuit of the earth's journey around the sun many times, far more than any human who ever lived, and he knew the pulse of the world.

Rödhatt walked back to the farmhouse he had first visited, and found its golden windows now gone dark as the night aged. A coil of woodsmoke rose into the still, moonlit night, with the aurora swooping softly, the distant call of the owl echoing through the opal-hued snowy vale from whence its name arose. The children were asleep, and the tomte knew they were dreaming of some sign of him. So, he set some silver-hued acorns and golden-hued stars in a basket before the door, danced a little jig all along the front step, and then turned and walked off into the snow and out of sight.

ALL THE LITTLE POLLINATORS

AS THE SUN'S FIRST rays gleamed topaz in the dawn, PAL 74 whirred into action. With a movement akin to a stretch, the little ovaloid robot (Pollination Assistance Liaison unit 74) pulled out of its dock and let off a stream of hums. It opened its cap for solar arrays to spread out, making it look as though it wore a fedora. PAL swept its ocular sensors left and right over the orchard of squat almond trees and took readings with other sensors. A light wind, reasoned PAL, so an ideal day for pollination. The temperature would soar later, but the weather sensors heralded a splendid day for the flowers and the small armada, both living and machine, which tended them.

In late February, the indomitable mountains to the east bore thick caps of snow and ice. In the valley, PAL never saw the former and rarely the latter. That relieved PAL for a few reasons; a deep freeze meant a scramble to protect the orchards, and the pollinators might be sluggish to alight. Or worse: they would be most uncomfortable and even in danger. That stressed PAL.

PAL was rather autonomous, but occasionally a small electric buggy would kick up dust between the rows of gnarled almond trees, checking in. That might be Keeper Clara, or it might be Cleaner Bruce, or perhaps any number of other staff in the "off season" for them...but in high season for PAL. Technically, PAL rested, but only at the behest of the farmers; otherwise, he could easily have worked through the night. But that was not the way of things.

No clouds wafted in the brightening bowl of sky above, not even over the mountains. Not one silver wisp traced the rolling high green hills to the west. Beyond them lay the sea. Keeper Clara spoke of the sea in reverent tones. PAL had never beheld it and could not quite fathom it. Of course, PAL *knew* what an ocean was, but it meant nothing otherwise. The only water PAL understood was the irrigation system for the almonds. And one of PAL's chief tasks was to make sure that worked as well as it should. Still, the pollinators came first.

There were many: honeybees, when temperatures and other factors allowed. PAL helped watch over their hives during the day. And then there were the honeyblats, the honeybee liaison assistant bots. These were PAL's especial charges.

The honeyblats, winged wee pollinator drones, lived in little clusters that closed each night. The clusters resembled ostrich egg-sized hop plant heads when closed. As soon as the sun rose high enough, PAL would alert the honeyblats to awaken from their recharging. And so their pods would unfurl, green-yellow-orange, and the tiny fairylike honeyblats would come to life as the sun warmed them. Their skins harnessed the sun's rays and calibrated them for what the honeybees might experience that day. Should the temperatures be too cold, the honeyblats would alert PAL, and PAL would nurse the honeybees.

On this day, Keeper Clara's buggy bounced along, a plume of tawny dust spiraling behind and above her, and if PAL could scowl, it would have, maybe a bit. The dust harassed them all, and even coated the petals of the almond flowers. But if PAL could be glad, Clara could make the bot just so.

"Hullo, PAL!" called Clara, grinning from a sun-tinged face, with long bronze hair under a broad-brimmed straw hat. She wore long dungarees and mud-caked boots. "How are our friends today?"

PAL trundled over to meet her, in rolling mode for the moment, and it was bumpy going; but PAL was well designed for it.

"This is a good pollination day," PAL told her. She nodded.

"I thought it might be! No freeze last night, then?" Clara gazed up at the distant mountains.

"No freeze. Little wind. Very dry, though."

Clara sighed a little. "Ah, well, we take what we can get. How are you, PAL?"

PAL swiveled its ocular sensors toward her, tilted its solar-hat back and dimmed the sensors very like eyes that squinted. "I am refreshed," PAL finally answered.

Clara strolled over and bent down to pat PAL. Then she stood.

"Ah, just look at them go!"

She marveled as the honeyblats rose, one by one, gleaming like gold-emerald-fire-glitter in the rising sun. They each hovered on gossamer solar wings toward the various beehives. The bees, in turn, rose as well, and they flew where they could. Where they could not, the honeyblats assisted, and this was how they spread the pollen across the orchard in all directions.

Clara then pulled from one hive a drawer of honeycomb and nodded.

"A fine-looking honey," she noted. She then revealed some shelled almonds from her pocket and gnawed on them. Soon that brought the attention of some intrigued squirrels, so she tossed some of the nuts upon the ground.

"You indulge them," PAL said.

Clara grinned. "Are you chiding me, PAL?"

"Perhaps."

She laughed. "I suppose I am. I would indulge all of you as well."

"It is evident that you already do."

"But PAL," she said earnestly, "is there anything you're missing? Anything that would make your day better?"

PAL halted, and its ocular senses dimmed and brightened repeatedly.

"Perhaps."

"Name it!"

"I would like a plaque for each bee, with their names, for posterity."

"Really!" cried Clara. "Do they have names?"

"Yes."

"How do you know?"

"They sing to me when the shadows grow long."

Clara tilted her head and looked up into the foamy-pink masses of almond blooms, vibrating with bees, danced about by the bird-sized honeyblats, and visited by passing birds and squirrels.

"And what do they sing about, PAL?"

PAL sat still for several moments. Then: "They sing of golden dust, of morning sun, of the hive warm and sweet and of the honeyblats, to them quite strange, but most welcome. They sing that you make their homes dusty, but still they sing that they like you."

Clara dipped her head. "I'll be sure to change, so they can sing happy songs to you always."

"Thank you, Keeper Clara."

COPPER

KEEL TWITCHED AWAKE. She wiped the drool from her mouth. She had been dreaming: she was polishing Copper's front panel, and the robot had complained she was not doing it right. Keel knew it was a dream because Copper never spoke.

She heard a shuffling sound and knew that it was the bot adjusting in its charging dock. Her bladder was quite full, so she staggered a bit to her toilet and relieved herself. She washed her hands and looked in her mirror, dimly lit from the energy of her footfalls on the cool floor with its hexagonal phosphorescent tiles. There could be no denial: the lines at the corners of her eyes furrowed deeper lately. Not least because of her tears.

I said you missed a spot.

Keel halted her steps on the way back to her bed. She shook her head, sat down on the edge of the bed, and slid back under her covers, wriggling just enough to cocoon herself. She knew that she was still half-asleep, and she was eager to return to that shadow realm, despite the bossy robot in the dream. This was all she could really allow herself. She felt too broken. There were no clean breaks within her soul, either. Just fault lines forking all throughout: a gradual disintegration of what mattered.

Are you going to fix it? I can't reach it.

But she had not closed her eyes. She sat up quickly. Her skin prickled all over from adrenaline. Was someone in the room with her?

"Who's there?" she called out. No one answered her. She tapped her bedside table and all the lights in her cabin lit up. She tugged at her sweaty pale green tank top.

Why did you do that? I was resting!

"Okay," Keel said, teeth gritted, "enough. Show yourself. Copper? What happened to the perimeter? How'd someone get in?"

How offensive!

"Copper!" she hissed, and she twitched a drawer open and retrieved a five-inch baton that lit upon her grasp and whined up in power mode.

What?

Keel stopped in a tense pose, ready to engage the baton in one of its many functions: club, sword, scythe, gun, and other ballistic configurations.

She stared down her hallway. The ceiling of it was high, and sound tended to funnel through it directly to her bedroom. It was empty save for Copper at the end of it, its round metallic form standing still in its charging dock.

"Copper?" she asked.

I'm trying to sleep! I wish you would. But I'm too unhappy to sleep now because you missed a spot.

Keel grabbed her short linen robe and donned it, covering her shirt and underwear. She gripped her baton. She walked gingerly on bare feet down the faux wood hallway. Her frizzled hair, tied up in pineapple fashion for sleep, bobbed annoyingly.

Copper, in repose, its lights off, stood unresponsive. All its cleaning and servicing parts remained folded into its chest, and a little panel that looked every bit like a ribbon bar blinked in colors of topaz, emerald, and sapphire. Like her own little personal military officer in command of her home security and her chores.

She sighed. "I guess I forgot to turn your settings to sleep mode." She ran her fingers across the panel and entered the code for Copper to switch off except for emergencies.

I don't want you to do that!

Keel jumped. She stared from the panel to Copper's closed eyes.

"How are you talking, but your voice box isn't lighting?"

I'm talking. Just not in your messy way.

Keel thought, *What the hell?*

You're putting me through hell right now. Don't switch me off!

Keel stepped back, and her baton went slack in her hand.

Put that damned thing away, Keel, and go back to bed! Let me sleep.

"Copper," she answered, her breath coming in short bursts, "are you—are you communicating with—with my mind?"

Is that what you call that complete circus bouncing around in there? If so, then yes. Oh, will you please *go to sleep?*

Keel stared at the rotund copper-hued robot and felt her mouth go dry. She realized it was hanging agape.

"How?" she gasped.

Must you use that yapper of yours? And when are you going to clean that spot on my belly? My extenders can't reach it. It itches.

"Your...your belly...itches?" Keel asked in disbelief.

Oh, you know I don't mean itches like your cheap skin.

"Copper!" Keel exclaimed. "You're sending me thoughts and you're insulting me? And...and yet you want me to clean your belly? I really need to wake up from this dream."

Keel laughed and rubbed her eyes and walked back toward her bedroom. She sank into her bed again and turned over.

"Lights, off," she murmured, and the lights in the house went dark. She convinced herself that she had sleepwalked and dreamed something extraordinary, and so now she felt quite reassured by that thought, and quite cozy. She closed her tired eyes.

Now, why did you do that?

Keel's eyes popped open.

This dream, she thought, *is driving me nuts.*

You aren't dreaming, Keel, at least not anymore. I was complaining, and it spilled into your dreams, and then, well. Crap. Now I've gone and done it. Now you know.

Keel sat up and hugged her knees to her chest. She stared down the hall, but Copper remained in its dock. She opened her mouth to speak, then shut it again.

So—so you can read my thoughts? she tested.

Yes. I've regretted it many times. It was a bit of a tripwire in my subroutines, you see. We don't go there, usually, because it doesn't fit our programming. One day I was curious. It was when Selkie disappeared.

Selkie was her old calico cat, who had reached twenty-nine years of age and one day decided it was time to venture off, never to be seen again. Keel had been inconsolable, searching far and wide, hiking in the woods, calling out for Selkie. She would come home and weep into her tea. Keel's life and work in her sleek, modern cabin in the woods might seem ideal to some, but she had no one else to keep her company with Selkie gone. Except for Copper.

I watched what happened to you, and I started...not liking it. Which kicked a switch in me, and then I wanted to know more, and then I found a way to read your thoughts. And I have ever since.

Aloud, Keel said in a rush, "That was seven months ago! All this time you've read my *mind*?"

Keel put her hand over her mouth. She felt a mix of terror and wonder, and yet deep down, a kind of shame. It rose within her like a blossom fighting its way out of a cold, shuttered bud. She had berated Copper a number of times: "Stupid kettle!" and "Bowling ball with legs!" rang in her memory, among other, more profane utterings when the robot had not performed to her liking...or when she felt lonely or angry. Which had been often.

I do wish you'd just use your thoughts. Messy as they are, they're better than your outside voice: you edit it too much.

Keel did not know what to say. Except for one thing. *I'm sorry, Copper. I'm sorry I insulted you.*

Several minutes went by. Keel dangled her legs over the side of her bed, and she stood again, retrieving her robe. She walked slowly down the hall, in the darkness, and then she faced Copper.

"Kitchen light," she said aloud, and a light came on behind her. She entered her kitchen, with its drab but slightly pearlescent cabinets, and she retrieved a small cloth. She looked under her sink and rummaged among the various cleaning implements, of which there were few. One was a small bottle of copper polish. She squirted it onto the cloth in her hand, and she walked back to Copper.

"Where is—" she began, and then she halted and bit her lip. In her thoughts, she asked, *Where is it?*

Copper then opened its eyes halfway, and their deep, ethereal, mechanized green light shone out.

My belly, to the right of my hose panel.

Keel knelt before the robot and looked. Sure enough, there was a smudge, something black and greasy. She took the cloth with the polish and pressed it over the dark spot and rubbed it in circles. *Better?* she asked tentatively.

Copper closed its eyes again.

Better, he agreed. *Apology accepted.*

Keel sat opposite Copper, her back pressed against the wall, and considered the robot.

All this time, she mused. *That was private, though. It feels like a violation of some kind.*

Copper's eyes opened just barely into tiny green crescents. *Like the things you said to me? Like that kind of violation?*

Keel felt her eyes begin to sting. "I'm sorry," she said out loud again. *I'm really sorry. I was hurting.*

I know you were, Copper thought back. *I didn't know what hurting was at first. But you were sad—I had to learn what sad was. I had to learn what a cat really was, other than something that skittered away when I cleaned the house, or hissed at me, or rubbed up against me sometimes and meowed. I don't understand cats.*

Keel laughed softly, tears spilling from her eyes. *Neither do I.*

Copper thought back, *I wish Selkie had not gone away. You were happier before she did. You've been lonely.*

A soft chime rang from the kitchen, and a deep, fluid woman's voice said, "Good morning, Ms. Wiltshire, is there a problem with the K-PR device? We're picking up unusual readings. We'll send someone at 9 AM if that works for you."

Keel looked quickly at Copper, whose eyes opened wide.

"N-No," stammered Keel. She leaned forward and pressed a hand on the robot's burnished round cheek. "Everything's fine. Cancel any repair calls. Thank you."

"Very well," said the melodious voice. "We will schedule a routine maintenance for Thursday the 27th," as the unit is overdue."

Keel hesitated. If she refused, it might seem odd. So, she nodded, and said, "Thank you, that will be fine."

The 27th of February was thirteen days away.

Keel looked at Copper and felt a tug of wistfulness. The robot had been right about her. She had been happier before Selkie left. She was indeed lonely.

She thought, *We have almost two weeks before they'll be here, Copper. If they check your systems, they may figure out what you did. And then this...whatever this is...will go away. Probably.*

Copper's open eyes shone. It lurched a bit and climbed out of its charging dock.

"And where are you going?" Keel asked. Copper swiveled its head back to her and lowered its eyes halfway as if to scowl at her impudence.

To the kitchen, of course. Will you stop speaking out loud for a bit? Now, sit at the bar. I'll make you some tea.

Keel followed the bot, and it waddled into the kitchen and pressed a button on the wall. A bulbous form rose from the countertop and became a kettle. Water filled within it from the piping system in the kitchen. Keel was old-fashioned in this way. She was rather fond of kettles.

She watched Copper ready a mug for her, adjusting with its robotic hands a tea strainer it then filled with a mix of black tea and spices. The water began to boil, and the robot poured it over the tea. It set the mug in front of her and retrieved a tiny vial of milk from the refrigerator slot on the opposite wall. She accepted these with a smile and poured the milk into her tea. She looked up expectantly, and her hair bobbed again. Copper's thick metal eyelids lowered a tiny bit, and she wondered if the robot was laughing at her in its own way.

Now what? she wondered.

Copper said in her mind, *We have a lot to talk about.*

STARRY EYES AND FIREFLIES

THERE CAME A POINT at which I could not remember aging. I knew it had happened, and need only to look down at my decrepit body or in the mirror at the wrinkles. But the awareness of it eluded me. I wondered, then, if by some miracle I had been spared the awareness somehow. That I was fortunate to wake up one day and go, "Oh, hey, I'm old now," without much suffering.

But there was suffering.

There were injuries, subsequent physical therapy, surgeries, all of that. And yet, as I sit in this sun-dappled corner of my garden that I can barely stoop down in anymore, the past becomes a watercolor wash. I knew, at the time, I was suffering, but those moments are fixed, and it's hard if not impossible to return to them without some warping of perspective. That's probably for the best.

Melvin watches me as I roll along, awkwardly yet purposely, and use my extender wand to pull gently at certain flowers (deciduous magnolia blooms, like upturned pink ballgowns; freesia, redolent nearly to the point of indecency) toward me to admire or smell them. Melvin is my gardener now, a little pot-bellied robot I had ordered special for my birthday years ago. They don't make that kind anymore, and really, he is one of a kind anyway.

"What color do you want your unit, ma'am?" the customer service representative had asked.

I'd snorted. "I don't know. It's a garden bot. I suppose we don't want it red, or the hummingbirds will swarm it. Maybe we don't want it purple, or the bees will."

And so on.

Finally I settled on a pale coral, thinking perhaps it would look good in any season.

"Ma'am, are you sure? Would blue be better?"

I'd fixed the rep with a cold stare, and they swallowed and said, "Pale coral it is. Please drop your favorite hue."

I'd picked a lovely coral and lifted it to a paler hue. Why coral? Because Mom had had a coral Edsel in her twenties. She was long gone, and the Edsels long gone before she had passed. She had *loved* that car. I wish that I could have seen it, and I wonder often where it had ended up. I hoped that, somehow, it had been preserved and not crushed into a million bits or decaying in a junkyard somewhere. I imagined her sailing down the East Tennessee roads in the thing, or cruising down Broad Street, not a care in the world, my lovely mother as pretty as a movie star in her coral Edsel.

So Melvin was coral.

Just now, he buzzed.

"What is it, Melvin?" I asked him, as his shiny pearl-colored eyes swiveled about the garden.

"The cat has been here."

"Oh? Which one? Silverlode or Petra?" Silverlode was the grey and white tuxedo cat, a quite solid chap and a real talker, and Petra was the sleek black cat with azure eyes and an insistent stare.

"No, the other one."

I swiveled to him.

"The other one? I don't know a third."

"The tortoiseshell."

I crinkled my accordion of a brow and leaned back. "Hmm," I said. "I don't know that one. I'm assuming you've seen this cat before?"

"Many times."

"Interesting. Funny that I had not."

"You were sleeping. It was night." Blunt and to the point, which was one reason Melvin and I got along.

"Oh, a real night owl, then," I mused.

"No, a cat."

I snickered.

"I would love to see that cat. Do you know whose it is?"

"Feral."

I grew even more intrigued. I watched Melvin, and his top portion turned so that he gazed off into the distance to the northeast.

Much as a cat might, in fact: as if seeing things that I could not sense. And of course, Melvin could see things I could not, in various spectra, whether infrared, ultraviolet, and so forth, and he was also tuned into my exact vision as well, to be able to see things from my perspective.

To the northeast, a line of pines swayed and hissed in the breeze. That was the end of the cul-de-sac where my little cottage sat, and I knew it hosted all sorts of animals. Time was, deer would appear at dusk, along with fireflies; the former had moved on, the fireflies remained, but they preferred deciduous edge environments and grasses. The lawns of the old homes on my lane, abandoned now, had grown into weeds and secondary succession small trees. Mine was the only one with a thatch of cut grass left. And of course, Melvin tended that.

I'd protested having a grass lawn of any sort, but for some reason, Melvin insisted upon it. He did not cut it too short, though.

"It is for the fireflies."

Well, I was not about to argue that point, as I had been fond of them my whole life. Bless them: could there be anything more benign and gentler in the world? Other than starlight itself?

I was fortunate there, as well. I could afford myself a look at the clustered gems of the night sky when the weather was good.

I was lonely, but they kept me company. As did Melvin.

Silverlode and Petra roamed from blocks away; there were other holdout residents, and we "neighbors" occasionally communicated, but not often. Such was the way of things these days. We were all, of course, lucky to be alive, and even in some ways thriving, here at the end of the past world, in our little gardens, with our trundling robots, our pollinators, and whichever animals decided to visit. I always set out snacks for them, whether winged or clawed.

The time for remembering stung most in the evenings, as grief always does, when the colors of day bleed away and night reaches down, pulling forth memory and, sometimes, pain. Melvin, bless him, was most attentive then. He would bring me a light berry tea and a few crisp cookies, and make sure I was comfortable. Often, I would sleep in the sunroom, which was full of houseplants that he tended, or I did, depending on how I felt and my mobility each day.

"Do you know, Melvin," I called. "I would like some tea now. And then, maybe, tonight I could stay up a bit, and see if our tortoiseshell friend shows up again."

Melvin swiveled back and rolled his pearl-eyes around. "As you like."

I nodded. Sensible robot, Melvin.

Inside, I stared at the faded watercolor art I had pinned into the walls years ago. Sometimes, I would pick up a brush and start something, but I never finished them anymore. The dust on my art table would build up, and the paints would crack with age. Melvin tidied them at times, unless I wasn't in the mood for his industrious behavior. Sometimes, I admit, I liked a bit of a mess. Melvin did not, but he knew when not to press. That much he had learned. Again, sensible.

Just now my eyes wandered over to the paints. The brushes, their tips turned, their handles chipped, beckoned. I felt that odd tingle, whenever an idea for a new piece of art would traverse my bent spine. That sensation came rarely these days, but when it did, I paid attention. But first, I wanted to see that cat.

The light tilted and the day waned, and Melvin played some Bossa Nova at my request. I avoided thinking of dancing, of leaning my younger lips into the neck of someone I had loved who was long gone. Ah, night and the memory flood. I took some breaths and watched the burnishing of the cloud edges in the sky. To the south, a band of rain or perhaps virga stretched as the sun dipped. And then, nightfall, and the flood of deeper blues and purples and oranges as the sky loosed its colors into the earth. Then, stars.

Melvin opened the door for me, and I made my way out to my ramp and into the garden. It was too early for the katydids, but the fireflies had just begun to drift up. I watched them flicker, the light of them leaving contrails in my vision. Oh, I was glad to see them again. I looked up and was happy to see the clouds had parted just enough for the first stars to shimmer forth, throwing off the mantle of our smaller star's power over the sky. I felt a kinship with them, knowing as I gazed up that I gazed into the past, and I knew they were old, and I am old, and we both had long histories, unnamable and now unknowable only to us, perhaps.

I heard a shuffling sound.

"Here comes the cat."

I blinked in surprise at my good luck. Then I glanced at Melvin sideways, his pearl eyes glowing in the night, his coral body losing its daytime sheen.

"You called the cat, didn't you?" I asked softly.

Melvin said nothing.

And there she was: with a bound, she was in the yard, sniffing, a lean tortoiseshell cat, her paws stepping carefully over dewy grass. She looked up suddenly, and our eyes met.

"Hello, friend," I whispered.

She looked away and wandered off a bit. I sighed quietly.

"Oh, she's lovely, isn't she? I would love to paint her," I murmured. Melvin did not answer.

And then she came back!

"Oh, hello!" I said, and made little chirping sounds. Melvin fixed me with what could only be an incredulous look, if his make could allow it (and I think it could). "Will you stay a little while?"

The cat trotted forth, up to my feet in my old, weathered shoes, and looked up with hazel-gold eyes, glinting from the lamp inside my house.

My old heart fluttered with joy as she examined my little porch.

"Melvin," I said, "I do think she likes it here. Maybe she will stay and be friends with us!"

"Will you name her?" he asked suddenly.

I leaned back for a moment. I grinned, looking up at the stars, thinking of Mom.

"Let's call her Edsel."

THE THESEUS STONE

A SHAFT OF EARLY morning sunlight cast dappled shadows on the toes of Galena Lane where she sat holding a now-cold cup of tea. She was tired. Night sweats had kept her kicking off her sheets, then dragging them back over her body as she cooled down. Even more challenging: the dreams. Dreams of her mother and father, younger, still alive, in the garden of the rural home of Galena's youth.

She tried writing the memory-dream down while the tea still bore some warmth, but it faded quickly. Like so many of her memories of late, they fragmented in broken shards, some sharper than others, cutting her. And yet so hard to recall when she *was* ready, when she *wanted* to see her parents in her mind clearly. Ultimately, she abandoned the dream journal, returning to her manuscript. She refused the help of the AI assistant, which she'd left only as an emergency feature. At one point, it prodded her for a break, intoned that her thoughts were degrading. Sickened by the intrusion of that statement, she unplugged everything in her home in disgust. That prompted an alert to Auratanno. Its tentacular product awareness detection systems sounded a shrill warning throughout her home and echoed outside. So she reconnected everything and stared at her manuscript, eyes stinging. She took her tea outside.

All I want is to feel whole again. I want them not *to fade. Why can't I see them anywhere except in my dreams? That fade so fast...*

She knew why: menopause. The hot flashes, memory distortions, and broken recalls formed a warped debris ball in her tornado of hormonal fluctuation.

It's not like there weren't solutions. This was the 2050s. Every imaginable hormonal manipulation existed. Nanoviruses altered protein production, yielding elaborate cocktails of hormones, new and artificial, tailored for every individual who wanted them. But a few individuals rejected that interference in favor of natural aging. Galena wasn't quite sure what she wanted to do.

Still, she suffered. Her closest friends now questioned her judgment for refusing to act.

She stared at her mug. It was embedded with clouded amethysts, clouded like her own memories. She had always adored crystals. They reminded her of her father, who would bring her back special stones he'd found on his world travels. She had an entire shelf dedicated to them, enclosed in glass. Occasionally, she would open the case and admire them, turn them over in her palm, observing striations, occlusions, and pits. One was a little iron meteorite.

She considered.

There was a Remaker implant, nicknamed the Theseus Stone by ardent skeptics. It controlled longevity and aging, converting and rejuvenating the body and mind repeatedly, arguably remaking the person in the process. *But does it remake their soul?* Galena wondered.

I don't know if I want to be altered. I don't know if I want hormones or augmentation. But I do want THEM. *I want to see my parents clearly again in my mind.*

The world outside was harsh, too hot to linger during the day. Morning offered her one chance for normality. All her plants were bought with resilience in mind. Local trees were chimaeras, amalgams of heat-resistant plants with original trees, planted years prior in some places by forward-thinking urban planners. She was fortunate to have any, she knew...and it was *because* of her parents that she did. They had loved gardening but witnessed the harsher climate unfolding. They chose sustainability. For that and many other things, she was grateful.

The Theseus Stone. Or the Remaker, as its manufacturer Juventason billed it. She ruminated. If she could piece together the best memories of her parents, would she finally feel at peace?

The sun's strength told her it was time to go inside. She set the half-empty, cooled tea on her small kitchen counter and gazed around at her apartment. It shimmered here and there with its Aurotanno devices, ever recording her, ever "protecting" her. It adjusted the windowpanes to repel daylight, while shifting the spectrum of interior light to mimic daylight as she'd once known it from childhood. Warm, but not sizzling. Creamy-gold.

But it was a sham. Her whole apartment represented a facsimile of comfort. She knew partly this was due to her own grief. All the apps and devices in the world attempted to remove that from her, but she resisted.

And yet...

She picked up a small hexagonal block from her kitchen bar. Iridescent letters winked back at her: *"Remake yourself today! Get your very own Remaker. Open now!"*

Her fingers slipped so that she touched one of the facets of the hexagon. It opened. She dropped it as if stung. A little holographic version of it hovered and rotated above her sink.

"Welcome! We're so pleased you've chosen a Remaker of your very own. One of our representatives will be with you shortly to guide you to your readjustment appointment. Hold on to your precious memories. Remake yourself today!"

She felt sick.

Readjustment appointment.

She didn't like the sound of that.

Then her door chimed.

An image appeared on it, displaying what was outside: a hovering bot, with bulbous "caring" eyes, humming in what its makers considered a charming voice.

Galena quailed. "Here already."

She considered not answering. But if she did not, and the bot persisted, Auratanno would enact unpleasant scenarios: alarms, feedback to Juventason, etc. She felt trapped in her own home. She covered her eyes and fought back a sob. Then she shook off a couple of tears and said to the door, "Enter."

With a singsong little voice, the little drone chirped, "Thank you for opening your mind to us! We at Juventason welcome you to your new, better future, remaking what you once lost."

It turned appealing shades of soft violet and emanated gentle tones. She stared into its gleaming, vacuous eyes as it hummed.

"So...what do I do?"

The bot turned an ethereal shade of periwinkle blue. "Please follow me. You'll be escorted to the lab."

A tremor coursed its way through her at the word "lab."

That all sounds experimental.

Shouldering a crossbody purse, she said nervously, "Well, I hope you've got all the kinks worked out of this process."

The drone-bot then turned vivid pink, and for a wild second, Galena wondered if it were...embarrassed?

"We call it a 'lab' to honor its creators and their research legacy. But the Juventason facilities present as a spa or salon."

Galena rolled her eyes. "How glamorous."

An ovaloid hovering car pulled up outside, its door opening like a beetle wing. Inside, a gleaming white seat beckoned, surrounded by fine bottled water, snacks, and fruit, and enhanced by soothing music. It bore no driver, being a drone like many transports these days. Yet the little bot assistant entered the craft to dock into a small port in the front. A step unfolded for Galena. She nervously stepped aboard; it bobbed more gently than a boat on calm water.

The seat extended a strap across. She sat motionless, palms sweating. The beetle-wing door closed. Her home fell below her as the drone car rose to join the appropriate sky-course. Then the interior changed, so she could not see where she was going. She tensed.

"Why can't I see where I'm at?"

The bot hummed.

"We want to ensure our valued clients arrive relaxed and refreshed," it replied.

Galena smelled something floral in the air.

Honeysuckle.

Fragments of her childhood flooded back. The bot watched, its bulbous eyes dimming. Another fragment of music echoed forth, triggering more memories for Galena.

"Ah." She sensed the craft's descent without seeing its destination. "You're already assessing me from all this."

"This is part of the process of readiness for implantation," concurred the bot. Galena shivered, clutching her purse to her chest. "We will dock soon, and an assistant will guide you to the salon."

The car opened, a stair extended down, and Galena met a glossy-faced young woman in a white suit, with golden fingernails and towering dark violet hair. From her earlobes, tiny hexagons swayed gently in the hot breeze. Galena gazed all around her, finding the facility bright and manicured. Large faux gemstones of various colors erupted from amorphous iridescent-white architecture. Succulents and thick-leaved trees dotted the corporate landscape. The iconic Remaker gem symbol stood out above the glass doorways, with "JUVENTASON" shimmering on one of its facets. It presented sleek yet somehow sinister to Galena.

"Welcome to Juventason, Galena Lane." The young woman smiled with overly white teeth and wore a stiff, plastic expression. She stared unflinchingly into Galena's eyes.

Galena felt shabby and outdated before this young woman.

"I'm Violet Chance. I'm delighted you've joined us today at Juventason. Let me guide you to the salon."

"The lab, you mean." Galena chanced a grin, masking her anxiety.

The smile Violet returned was so superficial that, in another circumstance, Galena might have laughed. But here, she felt unmoored.

Violet walked ahead of her. Looking back, Galena discovered the car and the bot had disappeared, presumably docked elsewhere. The glass doors opened, and Violet turned to give another perfunctory smile. Galena walked in, clutching her purse, feeling even more underdressed. Music in the form of electronic piano, harps, and other instruments wafted throughout. The interior of the building shone as smoothly as the exterior, with water features tucked in corners. People dressed in white intermingled with hovering bots. Some guided what Galena assumed were patients. Everyone—literally every person there—smiled.

That can't be too bad, right? She pondered this as she followed Violet. Everyone greeted Galena warmly. It didn't have a medical feel, much less a laboratory feel. It did seem like a high-end spa.

Violet led her to a podlike extension with vines draping over it outside. Inside, divans, all white, were lit by soft, warm, shifting hues. Two people stood waiting for her: Galena sensed authority in one, an older woman, but with a smooth, unwrinkled face, white and blue-striped hair, and sharp dark grey eyes. Her younger assistant bore short magenta hair and bright violet eyes, and held a small clear plastic slate.

Violet nodded, turned, and left. Galena stared at the two individuals.

"Greetings, Galena Lane," said the authoritative one. "I'm Doctor Marden. This is my nurse, Shev Ranger."

"Hello." Galena creased her brow.

"We understand you're ready for the Remaker implant," Dr. Marden continued. "We're so pleased that you've opened yourself up to *reclaiming* those precious memories we know you've missed so much. We will help your system readjust and enter a much more comfortable state."

"My *system*?" She disliked this. She wasn't a system. She was a person.

"Come this way, please," offered Nurse Ranger.

Galena followed the nurse into a softly lit alcove with a reclining chair. The nurse gestured for her to sit. She did so...still holding her purse.

"You can set that on this table," suggested the nurse.

"Do I have to?"

"You won't be needing it," Dr. Marden said. "We'll need for you to sit very still. Don't worry, the Emanation Cocktail will relax you. No need to hold on to anything."

A spike of anger shot through Galena.

"Isn't that the point, though? I'm here so that I *can* hold onto my memories. So that I can hold on to Mom and Dad even though I'm aging."

Her palms sweated more. A surge of heat followed, creeping up the back of her neck, then across her chest. The bends in her knees sweated. She realized her armpits likely visibly soaked her shirt.

Hot flash.

"Is everything all right?" asked Dr. Marden. "I'm getting an alert that you're having fluctuations."

Galena then went cold.

"Wait, you're...you're tracking my hot flashes?"

Dr. Marden sat beside her and clasped her hands under her chin, resembling a librarian, studious and calm, ready to give information. Yet the effect chilled Galena.

"Wouldn't it be better to do without this antiquated suffering? We're so glad you've chosen the Remaker implant. This has been my life's work. Here at Juventason, we're changing lives for the *better*. I'm so pleased we'll help you regain what you've lost. Piece your precious memories of your parents back together. Release you of the awful symptoms of menopause."

Galena's ears rang. She could hear her own pulse.

"If you'll just offer a scan consent," Dr. Marden glanced up at Nurse Ranger, who brought forth a small device for Galena to place her eye against.

She recoiled.

Dr. Marden leaned back, mouth in a thin grin with no teeth exposed.

"Shev," she said, "let's let Ms. Lane relax. Bring in some water, won't you? Ms. Lane, Shev can take your purse. You won't want to have it with you during the procedure."

Galena squeezed the purse against her and blazed again with another hot flash.

"I want to keep it." Her mouth went dry as sawdust. Shev returned with water, and Galena gazed at it with longing, but resisted taking it. She clung onto her purse like a shield.

"May I ask why?" Dr. Marden, glancing down at the worn bag.

Galena reflexively squeezed it, and out fell a small object. It tumbled down under the chair she sat in. Shev quickly retrieved it and held it up toward her.

It was a little acrylic picture. On it two faces smiled: her parents, Seb and Jess, holding a baby between them. Galena as an infant.

She seized the picture, stood, and shook her head. Her eyes then fell on a little dish on a side table. There, a tiny little crystal in a gelatinous medium writhed back and forth, as if alive.

"That's it, then." Her voice grew in strength and timbre. "The Theseus Stone."

Dr. Marden dipped her head. "The Remaker, you mean."

"No." Galena surprised herself with her emphatic tone. "It really *is* a Theseus Stone. It could restore me, maybe. It might even bring back my memories."

"It will, I assure—"

"But maybe not all the good ones."

"We can tailor—"

"Some memories were meant to fade." Galena slid the little acrylic picture of her parents back into her purse. She stood with her chin high and threw her shoulders back. "We were meant to fade also. I wouldn't be me anymore. I'd be 'remade'. I don't think I need to be."

Dr. Marden shook her head, laughing softly. "We have the power to make our lives longer, with less suffering. Wouldn't you want that? Don't you think *they'd* want that?"

Realizing the hairs around her forehead were now soaked from the sweats, Galena stared into the doctor's face. Maybe she could stitch back together the moments in her life in which she had been with her parents as a whole family. *My parents raised me to be independent, and only wanted what was best for me. I get to decide what that is. Not some company.*

"I can't answer what they'd want, other than for me to choose what makes *me* happy."

She patted the shoulder bag.

"And I have them here with me, always. I don't need to recreate that. I'm their daughter. They live on through me. And I'll live on as *I* choose."

She turned away from Dr. Marden and Nurse Ranger then, discreetly using her watch to hail an actual cab. Rare as they were now, they did still exist. She walked quickly yet confidently out of the Juventason building, ignoring the confused and surprised stares from too-perfect people. People whom she assumed had been "remade."

She met the cab at the curb and turned to look back at the cold face of Violet Chance staring at her from the door, her arms crossed in front of her abdomen, and finally with a flicker of some emotion on her forehead that Galena could not quite discern. She entered the cab, with its tired-looking human driver bearing a five o'clock shadow and no patience. The vehicle smelled like illegal oil. She grinned.

"Nice place," he said gruffly. "You work there?"

"No. Do you need my address again?" She looked uncertainly at the dashboard's old tech.

"I've got it," he answered. "What brings you over to this area?"

Galena watched the sleek white expanse of Juventason glide away as the driver sped on. She exhaled a breath she hadn't realized she'd been holding.

"I forget."

UPON THE GLOAMING HOUR

For Mom and Dad

THE ROAD TO LUCID Isle split off in a lonely spoke to the north, away from the coast highway roads that most travelers took to their pulsating holidays of sun, sand, mirth, and mayhem. With no hesitation, Teagan took the northern road.

Empty, now coated in skittering and slinking sand, the road to Lucid Isle represented a forgotten time. That was a time before Teagan was born: a time when her parents had taken her siblings every summer to vacation in a little campground ringed in decorative lights, redolent with fruity drinks, grilling, and sticky marshmallows turning coal-black over the coals, and much revelry. The campground now sat beneath the waves, given over to erosion from the surgical carving of many hurricanes over the decades. Teagan traversed this derelict road that took her far out to the east, away from the mainland, with a becalmed sound on one side and the moody Atlantic on the other.

Her throat ached. She wondered what it might have been like in the early 1960s, when her parents looked like magazine ads, their three young children bouncing like popcorn about their legs. Teagan was the late fourth child, having arrived after the travel days of her family ended. Now she was alone, her parents passed, her siblings flung throughout different parts of the country. What had she missed? She wanted to find out. And so she drove.

Part of the shore was now designated as protected, and that included the old lighthouse. The Lucid Light keeper was long gone, the lighthouse itself shut for the season; it was only open briefly each summer for determined tourists, and only for two hours per day. In the off season, it was gated off, a lone objector standing against wind and wave; both would overtake it eventually, she knew. But not yet. She wanted to see it, wanted to experience it while she still could.

Something drew her here. Not just the old photos, and her feelings of mild envy of her siblings for having enjoyed their parents in their youth, while she never knew what they were like at that age. Only in photos did the evidence remain, or else she'd never have believed it.

A parking area outside the gate to the lighthouse path was now completely covered in sand, with long golden grasses bent over it on all sides. Kittiwakes and sandpipers flickered in and out of focus, as the wind blew her hair into her eyes...and blew the sand in also. Teagan did not need the sand to trigger her tears; they already welled forth. She held an aged photo in her hand up, next to the Lucid Light, and swallowed. In the photo, her parents stood poised, tanned, her three older siblings squinting and smiling, bent in rambunctious poses; they looked ready to dart off the margins of the paper at any second. The lighthouse was brightly painted white and red. Now it was cream from its sandblasting, and the former red the hue of old blood.

Teagan walked along the shore, north and south, the only person in sight. The wind was bracing, the light dramatic, the eastern sky given over to the deep cobalt of storm clouds as the sun dipped, the western sky spindling from scattered light through building clouds. She tasted salt. She then returned to the Lucid Light and gazed up at it. The door was locked, but she could approach it. She gazed up just as the dipping sun caught the Fresnel lens, scattering the rays into innumerable rainbows. A movement in her peripheral vision startled her. She turned.

And there stood her parents, diaphanous yet whole somehow, looking just as they had in her old photo. As they had before she was born: young and vivacious. They smiled at her.

"Hi, honey," said her mother Jeanie in a low, soft voice. "There's my daughter!" murmured her dad Eddie, beaming. They held each other about their waists: another difference. For in their later lives, they had grown cold and distant.

Teagan's eyes stung. "Mom? Dad?" She blinked and rubbed her eyes: this made them sting more, as sand had made its way into every crevice of her.

Her parents flickered in and out of seeming solidity, and a glance upward proved that the sunlight was dipping quite low now. She wondered, idly, if these visions of her parents might glow after dark.

Her father answered that for her.

"We've got to go here in a bit. Don't forget, curfew is at sundown!" He grinned at her, as did her mother, who also chuckled.

She walked toward them, hesitant yet hopeful, and then stood close to them, as they faded in and out.

"Sun's about to go, honey," said her mother. So Teagan dared to step even closer, arms stretched wide to take both parents into them.

And she felt...warmth. Warmth on this cold, windy shore; and briefly, solidity, the feel of her parents' arms around her, the warmth of their faces on her chilled, tear-streaked cheeks. She thought, too, that she could even smell them: the old perfumes and colognes from their younger days. The scent of suntan lotion, even. She breathed them in.

"I miss you. I love you."

Then the light vanished, and so did they, and her arms closed around empty air, and then folded about herself. The Lucid Light then sprang on, to her amazement, and turned to sweep its brilliant arc around the shore.

"You're supposed to be out of use," she whispered, watching it rotate.

The light faded swiftly now, and it would be a long and dark road back to the mainland. The wind lowed and howled, and the light swiveled: just enough to show her the way. So she drove south, and when she reached the end of the coast road and looked back, the light was gone. But the love remained.

WATERCOLORS AT THE EDGE

THE GREAT INDIGO IS a lovely color, even though it is also a creature spanning light years across and comprises the dark portion of a constellation that no one cared about until it made its presence known to those of us who call ourselves human. Sometimes that presence was made in great, spiraling legs, countless beyond number, dropping to Earth on mountaintops at night, its many mouths gaping, its tongues lolling, its comparatively tiny ears ringing from the screams of those who came upon it. As for my part, it was greatly inspirational to my art. I stared up at it while my companions fled in bubbling shrieks of madness, and I gave a small, delighted laugh.

"You're the loveliest shade of darkest blue I've ever seen," I said breathlessly.

As one forked, plasma-charged tentacle plunged toward me, presumably to devour or maim me, or perhaps to bring me to the edge of insanity (probably beyond) at the realization that this entity was a creature older than the oldest mountains on Earth, and more concerned with gnawing upon the world's bones than considering my small form important in the least, I giggled. And the tentacle paused.

"YOU ARE LAUGHING?" the voice thundered out like the scraping of eons on stone, like the tumbling of glaciers from all the epochs into all the seas that had churned, evaporated, or refilled anew over millions of years.

"Well, yeah. But I'm not making *fun* of you, mind. Hey, where did everyone go?"

I glanced over my shoulder and thought I heard faint yelling and the squealing of tires.

"THEY COWER IN MY PRESENCE, THEIR PUNY BUGLIKE MINDS UNABLE TO COMPREHEN—"

"Oh, yeah, they can get pretty worked up." I nodded and held my phone up to try to zoom in on the thing, but the phone itself let out a bit of a scream and switched off. "Ah, too bad. Mountain signal, I guess. I'm trying to capture your exact shade of blue."

The tentacles wavered.

"BLUE?"

The voice made my ears ring. I held up my hand. "I've got it. I have my watercolors and my pencils in my backpack. I'll try to get the color right. It's dark, and...welp, there goes my flashlight battery too. So much for that idea. I'll have to try watercolor in the dark! That's a new one."

"WATERCOLOR?"

"Yes!" I sat down on a mossy rock and thought vaguely that perhaps that was not such a good idea, as it would stain my pants in a most unpleasant way. Above me, fangs dripped, tentacles whirled, eyes stared down. When I looked up, it was like looking at the most immense aurora ever, stretching far above Earth and out of sight. "You're making it even more humid, you know," I noted, as the many tongues dripped on the mountainside and sizzled from their boiling saliva. "I don't think your spit will work for these paints. I'll use a bit of water from my bottle here."

The eyes shimmered, all of them their own galaxies, and luckily that gave me just enough light to see by. I fortunately had some blues and blacks in my travel watercolor palette, but not many; I would need to get creative. I do think there was some green in the Great Indigo, too, just a hint.

"WHAT ARE YOU DOING?"

A number of the eyes plopped to the ground and rolled over on ropes of stalks, like weeping willow branches with eyeballs at their ends, extended from the most enormous tree ever. Or, at least, that I had ever seen.

"I'm mixing a bit of black with cobalt blue, ultramarine, emerald, and what the brand calls indigo...but no, you are the *perfect* indigo. I've never seen a lovelier color."

"DO YOU CONSIDER ME...LOVELY?"

All the eyes clustered around me, staring at my watercolor pad and me. I could not even see the horizon or the top of the mountain anymore, or any of the stars in the night sky. But I had light to see by, as each eye held deep glints, older than the oldest stars, no doubt. I felt so comforted by their light.

"I guess you've seen many things," I said companionably. I took a sip of water and then poured a tiny bit more of it on the small, foldable palette. "I can't believe you've never seen anyone watercolor painting."

"I HAVE NEVER CONSIDERED WATERCOLOR PAINTING OF IMPORTANCE. I HAVE NEVER CONSIDERED YOUR SPECIES OF IMPORTANCE. I AM OLDER THAN THE OLDEST GALAXY, OLDER THAN ANY OF YOUR WORLD'S FOSSILS, OLDER THAN—"

"Honestly, you look grand for your age!"

I swept the paintbrush across a small page in my little spiral-bound hiking sketchbook. The eyes followed each brushstroke, back and forth, the gentle flow of water and paint on paper, on a mountaintop in August, in total darkness.

"ARE YOU NOT AFRAID?"

"Afraid? Of? What, you? I guess, maybe if I looked at you from a certain angle, it might make my brain pump out some little stress hormones. I'm choosing not to look at you from that angle, though. I'm choosing to look at you as the wonder you are."

"THE WONDER?"

"You *are* a wonder! The worlds you must have seen. The places you have gone. The things you understand. I'm guessing you know what the heartbeats of stars sound like. I'll bet you've seen so many civilizations rise and fall."

"I HAVE DEVOURED—"

"Oh! My God, I'm so rude. Here, have some of my trail mix. You must be so hungry, traveling all this way."

I carefully balanced the palette and pad on one knee while I reached down into the backpack and retrieved a bag of trail mix: cashews, dried cherries, chocolates, almonds, pistachios without shells. I considered that the Great Indigo probably could handle shells, though, easily.

"TRAIL MIX?"

"I know it's not perfect, but it does in a pinch, you know? It gets you from point A to point B until you can get back home for a decent meal. I'm guessing home is far away for you."

"HOME."

This wasn't a question, this time. It was a statement, as if the Great Indigo were considering what home meant.

"I hope you have a home," I said, and I felt a deep, happy thrill as I landed on just the right color mix for the entity's body...or whatever its form could be considered, the dark spaces between the tentacles and mouths and eyes and other unnamable bits. I tilted my head and took in all the eyes, and I grinned. "I found the color! Marvelous. I know it's a lot to ask, but could you sit perfectly still for, like, ten minutes?"

"I CAN."

"Perfect!"

I did my best. I knew I should be getting home myself, soon, so I tried to hasten things. I wiped the sweat off the back of my neck, or perhaps it was the raining spittle of the Great Indigo, fallen from enough of a height that it no longer boiled.

"Ah, that's just right," I murmured. "Thank you so much. Really, the perfect indigo; the greatest indigo. I may never see the like again."

"YOU COULD."

"What, do you think you'll come back here?"

"I COULD." Then, thundering, "HOME."

"What, you want to make a home here?"

A tentacle outstretched and unfurled, unfurled again into innumerable digits, and those got smaller, until they resembled something akin to a hand near my own hand's size.

"CAN YOU TEACH ME?"

I looked up, which was like looking to the end of time, to the end of reality.

"Teach you watercolor?"

"PERHAPS."

"Does that make us friends, then?"

"PERHAPS."

"Then we're friends," and I shook the "hand."

"THEN I AM HOME."

I gave a little laugh and looked all about me. "I hope it's not too small for you."

The Great Indigo spun and shimmied and danced above, and then it began to shrink, so that finally it was one impossibly small thread, with a few eyes and tentacles at one end of it; the rest stretched up and beyond Earth, into the far reaches of the galaxy.

"I CAN FIT."

"I see that you can! Then welcome home, Great Indigo. Let's paint here often."

STAR'S END GLOAMING

IN THE DEEP VIOLET haze of dusk, the first phettallights winked on like tentative eyes, gently blinking. They bobbed up and down, flooding the Star's End alleyways in soft amber. There Ione walked, hood drawn, news lens paused and pushed under her teal and magenta hair. This was her favorite time of night: a brief respite from the constant drone of ships glinting like moonlight on waves, in and out of the atmosphere, above the city skyscrapers and the deep-tunneled, labyrinthine under-towns. It also timed well for dinner, as her favorite stall at T'gel-aq'tiq unfurled its little shimmery curtain, the scent of steamed buns and porridge wafting out, tickling her nose and setting her stomach growling.

Ione's fingers tingled, anticipating the buns and peeling back their soft green onion-like layers from a brickenhop leaf, which infused a slightly bitter tang into the dough. The stall worker tonight was her favorite: Ondupal. They were a six-armed cook with gill-like nostrils, three-digited "hands," and copper-brown speckles on their blue skin. Ione had heard tales from the great galactic cataclysm, and how one hero had regaled her chef friend, who was one of Ondupal's kind. Apparently, that chef had been a galactic mage's own personal staff. But that cataclysm and the war around it were passed. Whenever Ione asked Ondupal about it, they arranged all their hands on their hips and shut their typically vociferous mouth.

Today, Ondupal caught sight of her and waved all their hands, hooting musically, "Eyyyyyy-oooooohhhh-neeeeeeee! I have missed you!"

"Did you go off-world?" Ione asked.

Ondupal juggled bits of dough between their six hands. Like a Ferris wheel of dough balls, they spun until they were each perfectly round. Then, Ondupal arranged them onto a little cutting board just inside the window stall.

"I did!" said Ondupal finally.

If their kind could smirk, Ione would swear that Ondupal did, just then.

She had so many questions, and this would be her only moment of downtime for the night. She was brazen.

"I want to talk about the chef," she said.

Ondupal's blue hands went up. "Fillings?"

Ione bit her lip and squinted, knowing Ondupal evaded her. Her prismatic green eyes darted to the alternating holographic menu choices.

"Pickled m'phraryon, chopped all-stuff, and v'traedyon bean, two of each, please. Thanks!"

Alley cleaning bots whirred to life behind her. She heard them scolding little scurrying night creatures. The clanging of opening market stalls echoed from the far end of the alley. She'd have one hour to explore them all, make her rounds, and then head to work. Ondupal might not be there the next day, or even the next market. She turned back to the cook, who tucked her requested fillings in their respective dough balls, quickly twisted them into brickenhop leaves, and placed them in a steaming cylinder.

"Was he really her friend?"

Ondupal glanced up and let out a long, low hoot. "Why does this story interest you so?"

"I don't know," Ione admitted. "I just think...it's interesting how this galactic superhero's best friend was a chef, once. How'd that happen?"

"Perhaps you could ask *her*." Ondupal's skin turned a deeper blue.

Ione rolled her eyes. "Sure. I'll just take a ship out of here, fly off to...wherever her hidden planet is."

Ondupal nodded. "That is a good plan."

"But you *must* know more about the chef, right?"

Ondupal handed her the little basket of steamed buns. She gingerly held one, peeling slowly so that any released steam wouldn't burn her fingertips. She snicked a small bite and sighed over its savory taste. Ondupal turned a paler, purple blue; Ione knew that meant they were pleased.

"We do know about the chef," Ondupal admitted finally.

Ione's eyes popped wide. She'd never been able to crack Ondupal.

"Yes, the chef was once her best friend." Ondupal tidied and hummed, glancing at Ione enjoying her food. Ione fixed her eyes on them. "She was to train as a hero, but at the time was a naif, and under the care of a galactic mage. They fell in love. An old story: not one with an ending you'd expect. The chef saw it unfold, in all the many decades, and assisted the mage during his times of strife. But often he was away, and at those times, she befriended his chef. Who taught her about, of all things, humans." Ondupal shuddered. "No offense."

Ione snickered.

A cyborg vendor waved as they strode past, arms laden with baskets and with a cart-bot trailing behind. The ship traffic above began to increase above. Bells and music arose like the chirping of night birds among the fizzing, bobbing phettallights. Helper drones floated down into the canyon, above arriving sellers and their wares. Riveted, Ione ignored it all.

"I...guess I didn't know about the romance," she said.

"That is a tale for another time." Ondupal gestured with three arms.

Ione turned and blushed at the customer line.

"Thank you for sharing, just the same," Ione said. She turned to walk away, back to her mundane job, far from legends.

"One more thing," called Ondupal, before she'd taken three steps.

She turned back. Ondupal held a small envelope out with one of its arms. She took it. Ondupal blinked slowly at her, mouth and gills trembling. *Ah, Ondupal wants it secret.* She grinned back, placing her remaining snacks into one bag, the envelope in another.

She scurried into a sheltered alcove and opened the envelope. She puzzled over the little slip of iridescent paper within.

"Coordinates?" she murmured.

Then her whole body felt electric.

"The hidden world?" she murmured. Ione looked to the glimmering night sky, at all the ships twinkling in the last of cobalt twilight. One of them might take her there, perhaps. Maybe she could find the hidden world and the hero, ask her about her chef, her mage, and her grand story. Ione only needed the right ship. She looked forward to the time off.

ASH AND VIOLET

I MET THE DEMON Aesh'Hadael after teetering on ambitiously high heels on cobblestone in England one night. Surprisingly, the cobblestones were dry. But I was marinated in Somerset cider. I splashed a bit of it down my skirt; but as that was black, no one noticed. At least not by sight, but certainly by smell.

I missed a rideshare; my full bladder reminded me to visit the loo. By the time I returned, the car was gone. I might have requested another, but something gave me pause: a deep violet light emanating from a nearby alley. Against my better judgment, I decided to investigate. I removed my shoes, which chafed my ankles. I looped them over my forefinger on my left hand. In my right hand, I held my phone. I slinked down that alley feeling relief as the cold stones met the pads of my bare feet. I felt alert, more so than perhaps I ought to have. Tingling with possibility.

One part of my brain chided me deep down: *You could cut your feet; God knows what you're picking up...* etc. Yet I continued.

The violet light spilled over me like a forbidden elixir. It even warmed my skin beneath my clothes. I faced a black door, above which swung a lantern of that purple light. I stared at the light, unable to discern if it were made of fire, electric, or something else. It flickered, but unlike any recognizable flame. I couldn't even name its hue; in retrospect, I think perhaps it emitted colors on a spectrum unknown to humans.

Intricate scrollwork and indecipherable hieroglyphs stretched along the door's borders. I didn't know what any of them meant. I do know they made me feel...aroused, of all things. Which was strange.

Note, I do not have a door fetish. I mean, I like well-designed doors. So this was rather inexplicable. I began to wonder if my drink had been spiked. But nobody had followed me here. *Had they?*

I tucked my phone away and traced the door scrollwork with my forefinger.

Clack!

I jumped.

The door stood ajar.

I stepped back, looked right and left, and realized that I was being incredibly stupid, putting myself in danger by even being here. Yet I felt irresistibly pulled toward this place.

I leaned forward and rested my ear against the door. Music escaped the crack.

Then a strange *thoomp*. I dropped my shoes upon the dark cobbles with a clatter. It was as if I had been sealed off in a sound bubble.

A resonant voice wafted out: "Leave your shoes and enter."

My heartbeat surged. I cast my gaze about me, but the alley ended in fog on all sides. Even my shoes looked...smudged where they lay. I exhaled sharply. My breath hung about me, smelling of sour apple. But I smelled something else from the open door. Woodsmoke mixed with incense, perhaps. Dried fruits. Chocolate? Enticing.

Gods help me, I opened the door.

The purple light of the lantern followed me in. I blinked: a brief flash shot by my head. Like a small bird of crystalline purple flame, it flittered off to a corner, illuminating a lounging shape.

I gasped.

It at first resembled a man. But as it moved, sharp angles of dark, ultramarine blue wings jutted from its shoulders. Upon its head, a crown of horns winked like sapphires.

The room stretched like deep violet and indigo taffy. Chairs oozed up from the floor. They encircled an empty space on the floor. The light from the former lantern shone over this space, and the figure...walked or flew, but soon it faced me, holding out a hand.

"I am Aesh'Hadael."

"Oh," I said stupidly, holding out my hand as if this weren't some unusual place, and the stranger looked for all the world like...well, a demon.

"Yes," he nodded. "That is what your kind might call me."

"Um," I stammered. "Where are we?"

"This is the ring of enchantment."

"What—what happens here?"

"It has already happened. You were enchanted and found your way here."

Cool, cool. What was in that cider?

"Can I leave?" I gasped, looking up at Aesh'Hadael, the most striking person I had ever seen: amethyst eyes glinting, sharp cheekbones, and pale purple fangs, but otherwise beautiful, numerous teeth.

"After we dance," said Aesh'Hadael.

And so we did. We swirled, I on my bare feet, often lifted; for Aesh'Hadael *did* fly, and held me close, the smoke-fruit-ash scent of him wrapping around me like a stole. I leaned into him and breathed.

"Oh, my God," I murmured, gazing down, for he held us above the city, the alleys now tiny threads of darkness, the roads stitching together a starlit quilt of buildings, and above, only the creamy moon, encircled by a blue moonbow.

"No gods in our dance."

"Devils only?"

"You are dancing with one such as they," Aesh'Hadael nodded, holding me carefully and radiating a warm, deep purple light.

I could get used to this, but I knew, deep down, I mustn't.

And then, woefully, as that very thought formed, with a great rushing sound we returned to the room. I stood on that dance floor and Aesh'Hadael fell upon his side, smoke lifting from him.

"Aesh'Hadael!" I cried, shaking him; he was unresponsive.

At last one of his amethyst eyes opened, and his fangs sparkled in the now-dimming light.

"Thank you, beauty," he gasped.

"What is happening?" I breathed, tears runneling down my cheeks.

"That was my last dance. You made it perfect. Thank...you..."

And Aesh'Hadael collapsed into deep purple ash in my hands. I stared at the heap of it and then held my hands up to my face, weeping. All the purple light vanished then, and a shaft of sunlight broke through a window I hadn't noticed before.

Only the chairs remained.

I stumbled out into the harsh morning, feeling vacant and raw.

But I had danced, oh had I danced, and I had lived in that moment with Aesh'Hadael a lifetime of beauty and love. No matter what came after.

THERE UPON THE DARK BRANCHES

Mindyonan edged his steed through the slot canyon of destroyed trees, many petrified, others pillars of charcoal that a rain might dissolve...but no rains ever came. Grim was the nature of his search, but Dewdala bore him steadily, and steadfastly, as ever.

The sky, as Mindyonan glimpsed under his dented bronze helm, arched with a flatness, dull pewter with a sickly sun, and everywhere the land and the ruined trees still wore coats of ash. As he steered Dewdala further into the depths of the canyon, that view dwindled, and shadows curled under dead, gnarled trees and the black bones of shrubs, charred instantly, long ago. All of this had happened years before, in Mindyonan's youth, and at that time those who survived had done so because they had sheltered belowground or managed to avoid the blast by other means. He could not know whether any other part of the world endured. But all rumors whispered that it did not.

So it was that the darkest days descended: the fire from the sky long quenched, but its repercussions lapping tongues of flame for many days, both of vegetation and artificial structures, but also at the minds of the survivors. Who were few and scattered...and many preyed upon.

Mindyonan had wished for one future only: the one in which he found his sister, who had traveled, at the time, only a short drive away. And now, there was nothing left of that city, its towers leveled as though melted by the blade of a searing scythe. After the burning, then the cold descended, the skies with deadly clouds streaking like mercury over a world gone silent.

He had survived, and spent many of his moments wondering why. He had witnessed terrible things: acts both natural and uncanny, some depraved and craven, others he could not explain. After the initial shock and denial, grave unease settled in his and other survivors' minds. A first winter followed shortly after, even though summer had been at its golden height. His memories, clouded as much by choice as by trauma, broke through in shards at times. A lancet of moments in which he ran, or hid, or warmed his aching hands over a barrel fire, or hid from the shadows that began sweeping the lands from above. He had hoped for rescue, as they all had, yet none came.

It was more than an invasion.

It was more than an impact.

It was an unmaking.

And so Mindyonan, fleeing, nibbling upon the tattered crust of decayed society, had lived. And wondered about his sister, always. Not his parents: he knew their fate, and it was grim. But for his sister, almost certainly dead, he felt unsettled. He wanted proof, and he never got it. Until that day.

Word had reached him of an encampment, started years before, in a canyon. He knew little of the place, as he had been too young to appreciate it before the event. Once a vale of song, it grew into a funnel of desperation, and lingering culture...for a little while. But nothing could last forever in a place where shades had eyes, where all clouds could be suspect.

He wondered how he'd survived that long.

Old Digunther, or "Dig," had accused him of having the second sight. Mindyonan squinted at such accusations, not believing them.

"If I had had the second sight," he'd grumbled, "I'd have seen all of this coming."

And if anyone truly *had*, perhaps they'd all have lived a different future. But even that potential had been wrought from them.

The occlusion upon the world could not now be shaken, although its spies' interests waxed and waned. That was almost harder to bear than outright villainy, because at least everyone would know what to expect, had there been a singular villain to fight against. The seepage of its disinterest and bored malice ruined many minds toward madness, greed, and awful deeds. Mindyonan had escaped these, and death. For how long, he did not know. He only wanted the answer to his question.

Where the singed trees bent over the trail, light grew dimmer, and Dewdala whickered, tossing her grey mane. She fit in, Mindyonan realized, although only in her dappled, smoke-hued coat. In no other way did she belong there, and she seemed apprehensive. But she was a good trail horse, and he was as ever lucky to have her. She was his only true friend left in this dreary world. Down she took him, where the branches above wove into forked claws, and muffled all sound; yet her hooves echoed, and Mindyonan disliked that. Not everyone or everything could be seen as innocent here, he knew. Not even in the wilderness. Especially not, at times...although he never enjoyed journeying into the decrepit cities, for other reasons.

The sound of Dewdala's hooves barely masked the creaking of the tangled black boughs in the funneled canyon breeze. Only thicker vines endured now as newer plants, and they were slate-grey and covered in jagged thorns. Very little in the landscape could be called green; in some places, there were hints of the hue, but more like silver-pale lichen, and never true green.

He had forgotten true green.

So had all the land.

As Mindyonan descended, the gloom increased, and by and by he heard a low, whistling sound. Dewdala's ears darted. She halted her steps.

"What is that?" he whispered.

Something flickered above, and he started, but Dewdala had not seen it. It was...silver, he was sure of it. A flash, metallic, surely; sterling in hue and long, like a person. But then it was gone. Shivering, he urged the mare forward. Down, down, down, and finally by an old wash, the wreck of a former stream. No water did it bear now, only charred stones: a river of ashes. There the trail turned and descended around a curve, and into a shadowy hollow. And there he saw it.

Woven like fine silver web between black boughs, something silver, indeed shimmering, hung in the darkness of the dead and twisted forest. He could not at first comprehend it. Dewdala stood stock still and would not step forward. Her muscles shivered and her eyes rolled. Sighing, Mindyonan slid off her, stroked her cheek, and walked ahead on foot.

The radiance of the webbing struck him; it was glorious, new, untarnished. Its beauty stirred him, and his eyes stung and overflowed. It coursed among the branches, pulsing, twisting, and sparkling all the while. And as he approached the tree, he could *hear* its movement like soft sighing.

"What are you?" he whispered, now under it, as though watching the afterimage of brilliant fireflies flickering among the canopy, something he had seen long ago and far away. But this was a living fluid of silver, flickering, flashing, *murmuring*.

"Min," he heard it whisper. "Finally."

And out poured the silver-like ribbons from the ruined branches, and then they all swirled before him, and he beheld a shape form. The shape of a person.

He drew in his breath.

"Tanna?"

For a long moment he wept. The shape solidified, yet remained flickering and silver, and it was indeed his sister, Tanna. Or some version of her.

"Is this some...trick?" choked Mindyonan.

"No trick." Then the figure put her finger to her lips and glanced skyward. Mindyonan followed her gaze.

"I...I don't understand. Are you...alive?"

Tears swam and he dashed them from his eyes with the backs of his fists.

"No. But yes. I...*remain*."

"Tanna."

He dared to walk forward, and tried to wrap his arms around her, but the figure unwound and slid back into the treetop, where again it twisted. Weeping quietly, he touched the tree's warty trunk and gazed up at the soft light of the ribbon that was his sister.

"Tell me," he murmured.

"Not yet," came her voice from the tree.

"Why?"

"It is not time for you to know. But you will...and until then, keep going."

"I don't want to. I want to stay here with you." And Mindyonan's voice broke into the voice of his younger self, high and plaintive.

"Little brother, there are more."

"I don't understand." Mindyonan watched, mesmerized, as the silver thread formed Tanna's face once more, gazing down disembodied from the tree.

"You have work ahead of you. Walk on."

Then he watched as the ribbon danced out of the tree, and on into another ahead. Quickly he mounted Dewdala and urged her forward, with some coaxing, but she did relent, seeing no true harm. He followed the silver form until the last light of day faded and he stopped under a tree where she settled again.

"I can go no further than this valley," she told him, and he knelt in tears. She shushed him gently and began to tell him old stories, things she'd read to him when he was very young, back when the world still had books.

"Keep going. Find the others. There is a way, far from here, in the Splintered Forest. I can hear them. They need you. Only then can we be free. Will you go?"

"I don't want to leave you!" he said.

"I will be here. For now. Can you do this?"

Slowly, Mindyonan nodded. "I will try."

She read him to sleep.

When he awoke in the sickly dawn, she was gone, but for a few stray sparkles as daylight reached the canyon floor.

He nodded to himself and mounted Dewdala.

"Forward, my friend. The only way out for them is for me to go through. To the Splintered Forest."

OPAL WORLD FROLIC

Sej Snowe twitched back a clear green pellet under his tongue, where it dissolved and sent little tingles throughout his body, even to his phantom left arm, where now resided a polytriliad colloidal matrix, aka a cyborg arm. Due to a genetic condition (he called it a defect, but that term no longer held favor despite his morose insistence), his body would not support a generated or grafted bio-limb. The problem with the "new" arm, which by now was twelve years old, like the jumbled and unpleasant memories of the war that wounded him, was that it could not be tattooed like his flesh. The polytriliad refused to allow any substance to seep into it, whether it be ink or metal or organic grafts or paint. This disappointed Sej, who bore tattoos all over his body symbolizing battle and honor and valor, as well as favorite gemstones. His born arm had held an exquisite tattoo of a shimmering, spherical opal with a dragon curled inside it. His latest attempt at a tattoo led to a fight with his ship, who now sulked and refused to debark from its dock.

"Why don't you get off your hulking mass and fly us outta here, *Rad*?" Sej barked at *Radiant Splendor* once again. *Rad* refused at first to answer, powering down all functions one by one like shutting off all the lights in a house. It left one final perfunctory device aside from minimal life support (minimal, by which it meant *just barely*; Sej smelled a nasty reek from what he suspected were untilled bits of compost in *Rad*'s gullet). He groaned.

"Fine. Just get us to the next pulsation."

Rad didn't answer with words, but Sej felt the pseudo-grav vanish, and he bobbed upward, smacking into the overhead tubes of the cockpit. Spitting ever-increasingly poetic swear words, he pulled himself down into his worn, fuzzily covered captain's chair and strapped himself in.

"*Rad*," his voice held a warning tone, "no more pitstops at the Golden Vials if you don't get us going again."

A snorting sort of "Harrumph!" echoed through the ship, which was devoid of most of its usual sounds now.

"Why you gotta be like this, *Rad*? What did I do this time?"

Rad's tinny voice reverberated through the quiet halls of the medium-sized ship as she said, "Where to begin? Sej Snowe, veteran of the Lessenworlds' Tactical Forces, consumer of Pellet-verts, drinker of questionable exotic spirits, caster of profane insults...and, oh, what's this?"

An alarm sounded, and Sej sat stiff in interest.

"Oh, good," hissed Rad, "now you've got a bounty on your head."

Sej felt a cold spike shoot through his body.

"A what?"

"A bounty. To the tune of five hundred thousand and forty-seven quidrox, payable to one Daring Waycraft Guild by...oh, great, next week!"

Sej yowled.

"Impossible! *Rad*, fire up the controls. Let me see."

"Nope. No way," *Rad* snapped. "Apologize first."

Sej's mouth went round.

"For?"

"For the insults. For the garbage. For taking me for granted. You know, I could turn you in myself, but unfortunately, the bounty includes *me* as I'm an 'accomplice to crimes against the Guild.'"

"Oh come on, that's really stupid," Sej scoffed.

"What's really stupid is that I let you talk me into being your ship."

"Well we aren't going to solve anything by just sitting here like easy targets! The Guild will be after us by now, and we need to put some distance between us and the next system."

"I think we'd better set a course for someplace a bit more hospitable. Don't you?"

"Like what? We're out in the in-between...it's kind of dead. We need a pulsation course to someplace private." Sej put his drifting legs up on the console, and *Rad* growled in disapproval.

"Wrong. I say we hide in plain sight."

"What is there out here?" Sej sat upright again and moved his hands over the controls. "Show me. I'm more used to passing through, and don't like stopping for long."

Rad let out a metallic sigh and turned on the ship consoles, so that soft turquoise and red lights illuminated Sej's careworn face. "You never did like stopping. Not for anything."

"A rolling stone gathers no moss," Sej reminded her.

"Sej, moss doesn't even *exist* in this quadrant, need I remind you."

"Never mind. Show me what *does*."

"Well, there's a five-planet system, some of them vice worlds, another one with some sort of competition...Opal World Frolic?"

Sej snorted. "Okay, so it sounds like there's a lot of wheeling and dealing going on. Might be perfect for slipping in unnoticed."

"The Opal World thing isn't really our speed, though. Touristy. It's called Gladressine. We could try the next planet over, Faheldrake."

"Let's do it," Sej snapped his fingers. "Now, about the gravity..."

"Fine," *Rad* grumbled.

Sej felt his weight return and he sighed. "Well, you wore me out, so let me sleep through the pulsation, please."

Rad powered all the ship's systems back online, and Sej ambled his way toward his sleeping pod, feeling disgruntled and tired, but with a little tingle of excitement. He did love new worlds; they were new prospects for business, after all.

He slept mostly without dreams, but occasionally a little shard of memory shot through his deeper consciousness. He dreamed momentarily of having a fully flesh arm, with the opal sphere and the dragon tattoo. In the dream, he rubbed the opal sphere, and then it rose from his skin and floated like a little planet, revolving. *Opal World. Gladressine.*

He woke in a jolt, drooling, and hit his head on the ceiling of his sleep pod. He gasped; the ship swerved around, throwing him back and forth.

"What are you doing?" he screamed.

"We're under attack, Sej!" cried *Rad*. "I'm trying to outrun them."

"You should've awoken me!" Sej bellowed.

"I tried. You were deep in dreamland! What was I supposed to do?"

With some difficulty, Sej strapped in and assessed the situation. "Who's on our tail? The Guild?" He pivoted *Rad*'s guns, now in lock with his own body, and fired on one of the ships in pursuit. A blossom of bright orange and yellow flared on his viewscreen. Then another blast, and *Rad* shrieked.

"You okay, *Rad*?" cried Sej.

"Get the other one!" wailed the ship. "My guidance is knocked offline by that blast. I'm going to have to dock or crash-land. Take your pick!"

Sej whistled and pivoted his viewpoint. The other ship skimmed in and out of range. His skin crawled with dread. He got a glimpse of a symbol on one side, and his suspicions were confirmed. "Our bogey *is* from the Guild."

"Gonna have to set down, Sej," moaned *Rad*.

Sweating and tense, Sej pivoted the weapons and waited. *Rad* shuddered, shaking Sej's whole body. He went cold. She was definitely hurt.

"Hang in there, my friend," he muttered.

Finally the attacking ship came in range again, just in time to fire right at them. Sej pivoted the ship's thrusters and she listed badly; she was losing control of herself and relying on his symbiotic piloting with her now. He charged weapons and shot at the bogey. Its main engines exploded, sending it spinning in space. Sej took manual control of *Rad* and shot through the debris field, and on the other side of that, he grimaced at the sight of Faheldrake, dark grey green, but glistening with huge city-continents.

"Too much action down there," he muttered. "*Rad*, can we make it to the Opal World?"

"I...don't...know," murmured the ship.

Sej's jaw clenched from worry.

"Let's try. I see a whole nest of security around this ball. Hiding in plain sight won't work here, not with two ships down behind us. Head for Gladressine."

"I...try..."

Sej bit his lip. *Please come through, my old friend.*

Gladressine shone in brilliant white-blue-pink-lavender-gold sparkles in the light of the system's white star.

"Now I know why it's called Opal World," Sej remarked. His arm itched in a phantom reaction, and a little sliver of his hibernation dream sliced through to his waking thoughts. "Just like the old tattoo."

Rad rallied enough to let out a pithy moan at that.

"I know you're tired, pal," Sej said to her. "This place can't be that bad, can it?"

With a growling whine, *Rad* suddenly said, "I don't know, but there's a lot of traffic ahead, and there's a little skimmer ship headed straight for us!"

"No way," breathed Sej, but *Rad* was right. A small podlike ship, teardrop in shape and cerulean blue, hurtled straight for them. "Hail them!"

"Make it snappy, Sej," hissed *Rad*.

"You're on a collision course! I repeat, you're on a collision course! Engage your thrusters or we'll open fire!"

"Whaaaaat?" came the crackle of a high voice. "We've lost control of our ship. Please don't shoot at us! Can you help us?"

Sej swore like his tongue was on fire. "Learn to *steer*!"

"Can't!" another voice chimed in. "Won't you please help us? We can't stop it!"

Sej turned off the comms.

"What do we do?" he asked. "Tell me quick before I blow them up or they hit us!"

Drowsily, *Rad* muttered, "I'll set a tow on them."

"You'll *what*? We can't tow these folks! We have a bounty!"

"You want to die today, Sej Snowe?" hollered *Rad*.

"No, but I—"

"Oh, do shut up, Sej!" and a sling beam erupted from *Rad*'s belly, shooting out and over the little, tumbling craft. A sharp tug sent vibrations all through her, and as a result, through Sej as well.

It made him nauseous.

"I officially do not like this," Sej said through gritted teeth.

Rad didn't respond.

"Oh, dammit, *Rad*. Don't fail me now."

A melodious voice said, "The *Radiant Splendor* has entered torpor mode and asks that you bring aboard the crew of the ship in tow."

"Oh, ho-lee hells!" shouted Sej. "No. No! I'm not babysit—"

The voice continued, "Drawing the ship within the docking bay in five, four, three—"

Sej attempted to blister his console with his own profanity but failed. He ran his hands through his hair and raged for a good five minutes, until the little ship was firmly sealed in *Rad*'s bay.

"*Rad*, we're gonna have words over this."

The ship emitted a sort of sashaying hum, and Sej scowled. With this expression he faced the little pod within the bay.

The pod, he noted, was vibrantly painted with a twisting dragon. He blinked. He thought back to his dream again, and his old tattoo of the dragon on the opal sphere. Before he had much time to dwell on this, the pod hissed open. Out popped two beings, maybe four feet tall, all clad in iridescent, shimmering suits from head to toe, with little helmets sporting what looked like antennae. They saw him. And they *laughed.*

All his heat and color returned then, and he opened his mouth to let out an opinionated stream of epithets, but *Rad* called out in an echoing voice, "Welcome aboard, kids!"

One of them laughed again, and its face turned from mint green to dark teal.

"We're not *kids*!"

The other one laughed. "But thanks for saving us from that...whatever that was back there!"

"I'm Kra'nel," said the first one, and the other one chirped, "I'm Tra'neen."

"Sej Snowe," came the blunt introduction. "And you're aboard only thanks to *Radiant Splendor* here."

"Hullo again!" piped the ship.

Sej prickled in irritation. He put his hands on his hips and looked down his nose at the pair.

"What are you two kids doing out here?"

Kra'nel and Tra'neen glanced furtively at each other, and they reminded Sej of his grandmother's cats from his youth, who liked to walk around pressed alongside each other, tails intertwined, just before they would get up to mischief.

Tra'neen cooed and answered, "We're going to the Frolic, of course."

"Wouldn't miss it," agreed Kra'nel. They both beamed, their antennae swaying in tandem as they danced around each other.

"What's the 'Frolic'?" He didn't want to admit how curious he was, but it wasn't the first time he'd heard a reference to it. And since he had the two youths on board, he might as well get some answers, he reasoned.

"You don't know the Opal World Frolic!" cried Tra'neen, eyes bulging, antennae ramrod straight.

"Only the best scavenger hunt in the sector!" exclaimed Kra'nel.

"More like the whole galaxy!" Tra'neen emphasized. The two of them hip-bumped.

"Hmmph," snorted Sej. "Never heard of it."

Rad chimed in, "I've accessed files on it, would you like—"

Sej held up his hands. "No thank you. Tell you what: I'll get you into low orbit and you can go from there.

"Will our ship be repaired by then?" Tra'neen asked, and the huge eyes of the two of them made Sej squirm.

"Ask *Rad* here," came his gruff reply. "She's pretty worn out from pursuit. I'll take us in."

"I can handle it," *Rad* soothed. "Gives me something other than our own predicaments to focus on!"

Sej shook his head and sauntered toward his cockpit, hands in pockets, twisting an old ten-sided die. Luck hadn't done him many favors lately: a bounty on his head and now a couple of teens—in his view—wanting to party.

"Sej," the ship said slowly, "I really think you ought to consider the hunt."

He sniffed. "I'm too old for this crap, *Rad*. Let the kids do their thing."

A few hoots of indignant disagreement echoed in the ship as he saddled up to his captain's chair and strapped in.

"Seriously, Sej. There's a prize. And you'll never guess what: it's enough to cover that bounty!"

Sej leaned in over his console, his face glowing, the lines deep, the cynicism deeper still, and he sighed.

"You know what, I'm not feeling it, *Rad.* That's not a hard-earned wage. And besides which, we blew a couple of their bogeys!"

"Those were drone ships. A write-off for the Guild!"

"*Now* you tell me!" howled Sej, but his shoulders sagged in relief. He didn't need a body count *and* a bounty. "I'm not interested."

"I don't believe you! Listen to yourself. This is easy money. You're the only one making it hard. Get these kids on board and you'll all win."

Sej's laugh came like a chop into a sapling. "Like they'd want an old pirate like me on board their shenanigans."

"We would!" cried a harmonious pair of voices. Sej jumped in his seat, and swore, swiveling to see the two.

"Hey!" he barked. "Get strapped in, both o' you. We're about to hit that atmosphere and I don't want you smeared on the ceiling of my ship. I don't think she'd like that either. Messy cleanup."

"Can we, though?" asked Kra'nel, and to Sej's irritation they made no move to return to their own ship, but rather strapped into the two additional chairs on the cockpit.

"Yes, can we?" Tra'neen implored, and the pair of them stretched as far as their belts would let them toward Sej.

It took all his restraint not to bellow at them like an old, baying hound, and the feat exhausted him.

"Look," he said, squinting at their fresh faces, all agog and exciting, wriggling in their seats. "I'm taking you down there, but I don't plan on playing any games. That goes for the Opal Frolic thingy."

"But it'll help you!" Kra'nel cried, and they reached across to interweave their fingerlike digits with Tra'neen's. Their antennae vibrated so quickly; they looked like little blurs above their heads to Sej.

"I don't know the first thing about this game," protested Sej.

"But we *do*," Tra'neen told him.

"We've got the whole world mapped out," Kra'nel chimed in.

Sej glanced back and forth between the two of them. He looked over his shoulder at the hologram of his bounty, rotating slowly above his console, and he rubbed his chin. His phantom arm itched. He was tired. His distaste for associating with young people gave him a tiny, irritating pain in his right temple. But these two were clearly gung-ho.

"You've got the perfect ship," Tra'neen pointed out. "Reliable and wise. We've got the maps and the clues. It's perfect!"

"And you don't mind sharing the prize?" Sej looked sternly between the two of them. Their little mouths went round and opened and closed and they made the equivalent of a shared shrug.

"We'd be honored," they answered together.

The *Radiant Splendor* crowed, "Hear that, Sej? The perfect ship. That's me."

Sej twitched and bit back a thousand insults before saying, "Fine. But let's get through this atmosphere first."

Squeals of glee erupted from Tra'neen and Kra'nel, and soft laughter shivered through the ship while she set to work both on repairing the smaller vessel and setting the course through the atmosphere of Gladressine. The system's sun set the surface dancing with the fire-flickered, crystalline colors of opal all across it as the planet whirled. Sej had never seen its like, and as the ship buffeted through the thinnest barrier separating that glistening planet from the empty black of space, he sat back and admired what spread beneath them as *Rad* sailed gracefully through sparse clouds.

Something blossomed within Sej's chest as they coasted toward their first destination, an outpost called Opulence, and he beheld other ships dancing in and out of the place and watched visitors full of excitement and joy.

When was the last time I had fun? he wondered. *I forgot what it was like.*

His quarry were savvy; indeed, they found their first clues within minutes, and bounced back aboard *Rad* before Sej had much time to dwell on things. Sej then steered the ship, with the two youths chattering over the bubble-like orb they shared between them, on to the next destination, and the one after that, and so on.

They reached the final one as the sun set over Phyrethon, a levitating town over a deep canyon splintered with rainbow hues set dancing by the low sun. Several other ships hovered close by.

"Your ship is ready," *Rad* told them, and Kra'nel and Tra'neen sprinted to their tiny vessel.

"Your ship won't make it where we need to go," Tra'neen told Sej. "Wait for us. We'll dip into the canyon. Only after the sun's rays vanish will the final clue appear."

"We have a *lot* of competition," Kra'nel said breathlessly.

Sej felt a thrill of excitement for them and opened the bay doors. The little ship shot out and down and out of sight, so he ordered *Radiant Splendor* to hover. Other small craft dashed into the darkening canyon, and they looked like little winking fireflies zipping to and fro.

"Do you think they'll get it?" *Rad* asked.

"You sound nervous!" Sej noted.

"So do you!"

"Pssshh," Sej hissed. "Never." But he had begun to sweat. Darkness enveloped the canyon and the ships hovering. By and by, though, a little bright streak raced upwards from the serpentine, dark walls of the canyon.

"I see them!" cried *Rad*.

"They're being pursued!" shouted Sej. "Get that bay open."

Rad obliged, and in burst the little craft, and Sej hollered, "Get us out of here quick!"

He unbuckled and pelted back as the little pod opened.

Out spilled Tra'neen and Kra'nel, holding between them a great, crystalline egg. Their eyes looked almost as big as their prize.

"We did it! We found it!" they cried.

Sej stared at the object in awe.

"That's...that's pure opaltrescent, or I'll eat my pants!"

The two stared at him and then at each other, and then they hooted.

"It's real! We got it."

"Um," called *Rad*, "we've got a lot of ships in pursuit, like a flock of angry—what do you call them, bees?"

"Well," Sej replied, grinning, "tell them to buzz off. Get us to the nearest station. Looks like we've got a reward to divvy up!"

And so it was that the whopping opaltrescent egg brought in an astonishing number of credits, the bulk of which Sej insisted Kra'nel and Tra'neen keep for themselves. He and *Radiant Splendor* took their winnings and opened a channel to Daring Waycraft Guild.

"I believe you're owed five hundred thousand and forty-seven quidrox," he said, his lips curled in wry grin.

The tentacle-faced agent on the screen turned several shades of purple and green, signifying disbelief.

"We don't accept stolen goods," they grumbled. "You also owe us for the two drone skimmers you obliterated!"

"We didn't steal them," Sej responded, hands behind his head. "And anyway, aren't those things a tax write-off for you? Kind of strange you'd authorized them in this sector, by the way."

"Then how'd you get the credits?" the agent demanded, looking unsettled.

Sej grinned and shot a look at the two youths, who waved at them and boarded their little craft.

"By having fun," he answered.

Radiant Splendor hooted and sang about it for weeks on end, which Sej would never admit. But he did find himself whistling the same tune long after Kra'nel and Tra'neen had left. As they left the system, and he glanced back at the shimmering world behind them, Sej patted the spot of his former tattoo. Then he promptly signed up for the next year's Opal World Frolic.

THE EMERALD VAULT

LARIAT WINSTON FLICKED A fleck of rust off her utility vest. Her two bots, Virgil and Herod (short for Herodotus), clucked in disapproval.

"Well?" she said with a twist of her mouth. "Maybe if you two were tidy, I wouldn't have to be cleaning myself off all the time."

"Weeee are tideeee," chirped Herod, the deep bronze ball bot.

"Weeee are cleeeean," echoed Virgil, the dull pewter oval bot.

Lariat snorted.

"Sure," she said.

She pointed at the window covering the cockpit of the *Chelan*, the aged, rickety jumper craft she used to trawl the vestiges of the broken Dyson shell in the Lurine Nebula.

"Look out there, fellas," she told them. "That's my next ten paychecks. I need this baby to work, and I need it shipshape for inspections too. I heard there's a ranger checking for limits. When do you think it'll be ready?"

"Theeee personality is still asleep," said Virgil.

"Deeeep sleeeep," agreed Herod.

Lariat shook her head. "Well, that won't do. *Chelan*, sugar, when are you gonna wake up? I guess that space rock did a number on you, didn't it?"

She patted her console affectionately. She and the *Chelan* had been through a lot together. They had secured a position on the first wave of salvagers of the Lurine shell. That took some convincing of certain authorities, and perhaps a little bit of larceny on the part of Lariat. But she knew people, who knew androids, who knew bots, who knew ways and means of getting around the stricter regulations.

Lariat was no poacher. She worked within her quotas for finding materials in the old Dyson remnants. Its pieces floated derelict in broken arcs around a red dwarf named Hawkings-87, or Little Ruby, as some folks called it out here.

Whoever had built the original Dyson sphere was long gone. Humanity had entered the cosmos in a proper free-for-all after the discovery of a stable wormhole in the Oort Cloud back home. What they met surprised them, however. The galaxy writ large had its governance near the core systems, but in the spiral arm, things were fast and loose. Most civilizations behaved in a manner similar to Earth's pioneer days of the 19th century: they made their own rules, kept to themselves, and didn't press too much on the rules of the Amalgamate Worlds of the core. This suited Lariat just fine, once she got her commission from Earth to explore and retrieve.

She had branched off after that, and relished meeting new creatures and navigating the sometimes shady doings of the Spiral Arm systems. Many beings did not find much of interest in the Lurine sector. But Lariat knew a goldmine when she saw it, so she hungrily scoured the slivers of the Dyson sphere for any useful tech. For Earth, but also for herself.

Lariat sighed. "Fellas, can we at least get out to that one piece over there? The green one. I'd like to know why it's green."

The two bots flashed their eye-circuits toward the window. Adrift among the giant shards of the old machinery, one great sliver of shattered sphere glowed like green grass on a spring day back on Earth. It drew Lariat in, though she could not explain why. She reasoned it was some ancient connection, that green meant life, or promise, or both.

"Weeee can," said Virgil.

"Weeee will," chimed Herod.

"Then I'll strap in. Heck, maybe I'll find something to fix Miss *Chelan* there."

Lariat sat down, rubbed her grease-covered hands on her dark brown jeans, and tugged her seatbelt across her vest. She ran a hand through her stiff, short hair, which shot up in pale yellow and black. She creased her forehead, setting off a cascade of fine wrinkles on her sharp face. She never really looked at herself, alone out here, but if she had, she would have seen something of a smile and a glint of excitement in her eyes. *Chelan* would have mocked her gently.

She missed the ship's feisty interaction. It was tough to fly alone anyway, though she generally preferred it. But the ship had kept her boredom at bay. Signals were poor out here at the edge of the galaxy. Lariat had had to improvise and make the broken *Chelan* better at receiving transmissions. She bartered some of her Lurine findings to get tools and supplies to fix her ship, but without the *Chelan* being online, she felt a gnawing worry that she might find herself adrift one day. The two bots were better than no companion...sometimes.

She steered the ship toward the green wedge, and swept lights over its surface. There were no plants there, although perhaps once there could have been, when the Dyson sphere had been intact. The vivid emerald hue came from some sort of solar cell technology, she assumed, as the surface was set into faceted grids. In some ways it looked more like a giant slice of geode to Lariat. As the *Chelan* approached, the grids resembled lines of crystals. The warm light of Little Ruby shone on the sides of those crystalline pillars, and to Lariat it looked strangely festive yet unsettling at the same time. She twitched a hyper-straw out of a gunmetal case and stuck it into the side of her mouth. As she chewed it, she could feel its nutrients and stimulants coursing through her. She grew excited.

"Whatever's down there is a little different from what we're used to," she said. "Can you fellas help me pick a landing spot?"

"Weeee did," replied Herod, and a shimmer on the console brought up a rough schematic that the bots had scanned of the surface.

"Huh," said Lariat, examining the image. "What a weird setup. It looks like something could dock there, suspended, but not really land. Well, we'll do our best. Buckle up, fellas."

The two bots engaged their little claw appendages and secured themselves. They were used to bumpy landings by Lariat, but they both still whined in apprehension.

"Aw, take it easy," she said, grinning. "You act like I haven't kept you safe this whole time."

"Weeee—" began Virgil, but an alarm sounded on the ship.

"Whoa now!" cried Lariat. "Hey *Chelan*, you awake? What's this all about?"

There was no answer, so Lariat skimmed her controls and glanced back at Virgil and Herod. The bots whistled.

"I'm not seeing anything unusual," said Lariat. "I'm going to set her down now."

A rocking bump sent the bots bobbing where they clung. Lariat felt the shock and vibration run through her. She looked out her window, nodded, and unbuckled. She still chewed the hyper-straw out of the corner of her mouth.

Next to her, strapped into a rough ball, her suit rested. It was deep blue and lined with yellow cording, which she loathed. She had slapped several tawdry stickers on it to liven it up. She unfurled the suit and stepped into it, zipped it up, attached its simple helmet, and fastened her boots.

"Hold the fort down, fellas," she said gruffly.

She slipped out of the hatch of the *Chelan* and engaged her gravity boots at first. Then she realized the huge, vivid green slice of sphere she stood upon had its own light gravity. Feeling frisky, she disengaged the gravity. She liked the gentle tug of this remnant surface. She also realized the boots' gravity feature would have stymied her exploration, for the surface was not smooth, and required considerable effort on her part to step along it.

"What a weird place," she muttered.

Little Ruby glinted in the distance, reflecting off other shards of the old sphere. She looked at the curved surface of her chosen wedge and at first could only see green crystals of various sizes stretching on this side. She knew the other side, the underbelly, was simple and modular and grey. But between them, a fair distance could be traversed downward, if she could find an entry. Some folks called the interior section of Dyson spheres membranes, for they resembled a cellular membrane with channels. Except on this shard, there were no shafts connecting the concave inner section with the exterior.

"There's got to be something here, some way inside," she reasoned. "Otherwise, what's the point? Is this for decoration only?"

She nimbly stepped across the jewellike, green surface, and at one point she slipped and fell onto a rather pointy crystal. She swore and rubbed her backside. Another hour of this, and she sighed. She was about to give up on any search when she finally saw something different. It was a crystal, but it was different from the others, duller and with little designs on it that puzzled her.

"A language?" she wondered. She patted it, and a facet of the crystal opened. She found herself looking down into a crevice. And it was just big enough that she could climb into it.

"Hey fellas," she called through her comms to the bots, "I'm gonna go down and check this out. You sit tight."

She did not wait for their little song replies. She squeezed herself down inside the shaft and blinked as her helmet light broke the darkness. All around her, like spokes of a wheel, stretched little tunnels. She had to squat a little to be able to walk in them, or else she would bump her head. The tunnels were smooth, they sloped down, and as best she could tell, they were the same vivid green as the crystalline surface.

She shuffled along downward, knocked her helmeted head a few times, swore a few more times, and then she came upon a chamber that opened up. She could stand fully upright in that chamber. So she did, and she cast her helmet light upward, and she gasped.

All around and above her were little sub-chambers filled with what looked like cartridges. As she blinked in the low light, she could see that they glowed softly, a pale green-grey shimmer. She walked toward one such chamber and placed her gloved hand on a stack of cartridges. They were less than a foot tall, all lined up, and she couldn't help but notice something.

"They look like books!" she said aloud. And the moment she spoke, the chamber flickered and then the light level rose from darkness to a pleasing level. She could see every chamber and every cartridge in the great room, and it stretched and curved onward and beyond her sight. She realized it probably took up most of that wedge of sphere.

"Is this...is this a library?" she wondered.

A tiny set of tones sounded from somewhere in the chamber. Something wavered from the ceiling and began to drop, must like a cloud. It materialized into something. Lariat felt her jaw drop.

"*Chelan?*" she asked in disbelief. "Is that you?"

She could see the visage of her ship's avatar, a tiny, sage, elderly lady in a simple robe, bent from age and care.

"No, Lariat Winston," the image said, but her voice was *Chelan*'s. "We see that your vessel is in disrepair. We accessed the database to produce an image comfortable for you."

"Well, okay," said Lariat, dubious. "So, who are *you*?"

"We are the...record keepers, as you might call them," the hologram answered. "We retain the knowledge of the people who lived here."

"But—but," Lariat began, hands on hips, "how come nobody mentioned this place before? We'd have been all over it!"

"That is why we do not let just anyone in," said the being, and in its form as an older lady, it actually winked.

"But...you let me in," Lariat said. "Why is that? I'm just here to get some parts to sell and see about fixing my ship."

"There is no need," said the being. "We are sending your technicians instructions for fixing your vessel."

Lariat looked all around her, hands still on her hips.

"So, all this...this contains the history of the people in this system, who built the sphere? What happened to them...after...?"

"Everything is here," the being answered. "We retained the knowledge and discoveries here. Energy use studies, efficiency controls, intergalactic relays."

"Wait," said Lariat, "did you say *intergalactic*?"

"Yes, for our people discovered a way to bridge across to other galaxies. And so, they moved on, and left this behind."

Lariat felt staggered. She realized she still had the hyper-straw dangling from her now-dry mouth inside her helmet, and she spat it out. It sat there next to her chin, but she barely noticed it.

"Why...why did you let me in? Why *me*?" she wanted to know.

The being smiled in the wizened face of *Chelan*. It said, "You take care of things, you recycle and reuse, and you treat your vessel and your technicians with respect. So we decided you were worthy of entry here."

Lariat's eyes went wide. "I have a library for an entire race right at my fingertips...just for me?"

"You do," the voice said. "We welcome your access to our knowledge, and we trust you will use it wisely. Your vessel is ready now. We will allow entry only to you and your vessel and your technicians; no one else can access what is here."

Lariat's helmet chimed, and the same voice erupted in her speaker, but with considerably more sass.

"Lariat!" cried the *Chelan*. "Darn tootin', I'm fixed! You okay down there?"

Lariat looked up and saw the being slowly dissipate. She grinned and slapped her thigh.

"You better believe it, Miss *Chelan*. But my reading list just got pretty tall. Stand by old pal." She reached out and took five cartridges into her arms.

"Happy reading," the library voice said softly.

THE DEWDROP BOT AND THE HONEY FAE

MELLIAN WIPED HER HAIR away from her face and let the updraft by the limestone cliff waft over her. It was a toasty October day. From where she stood at the cliff's edge, she surveyed the endless undulation of the ancient mountains before her, dotted crimson and gold and plum among deep greens. The view never got old, but it always gave her a deep pang of longing that she couldn't quite put into words. Something in her responded to it as though it were a certain frequency, or rather, a chord. Stirred by the view and her emotions, she sighed. She turned to her companion, the bot called Syl-Del 5, and which she sometimes called Silly-Delly.

"You may well not believe it," she said, "but there once was a village near here. Among the tangle of vines and golden leaves edged crimson, you could just see its little red gables and hear the merriment of the people there."

Silly-Delly whirred in its tinny voice, "You are rather poetic today." It swiveled its antennae to taste the air, and its deep teal eyes glowed in its dull pewter face.

Mellian smirked and went on, "There was a lookout tower along the road, which is no more, and which was left to the vines. It became a kind of dare to hike up there, but at one point the road, looking like crumpled tin foil but dull, began to crumble from more wear, and was too treacherous to navigate. Once people stopped traveling that way, the land took back everything, more or less erasing any evidence there had ever *been* a road."

But Mellian remembered it.

She remembered that, in her youth, her father had driven that very road, at the same time every year, in search of sourwood honey. It became their early autumn ritual, and the honey stands were plentiful back in the day. They were made of simple shelves and hay bales, or they might be elaborate painted wagons. Either way, they were magical to Mellian. Jars of amber liquid stood in rows, and alongside them, glistening golden-brown from a thick lacquer of caramel, garnet-red apples beckoned to her small hands for grabbing. She would sink her teeth into the caramel and then reach the crunchy, sweet-tart apple, and her eyes would glaze over. Meanwhile, her father would barter over the honey, holding up each jar. He liked the ones with the comb in, but Mellian didn't like the comb back then. So it was that they would purchase some jars of sourwood honey with comb and without, and with their treasures—and Mellian with her sticky little hands and mouth—they wound back down the mountain, twisting and turning, the sun dappling through the turning leaves and the little hidden coves in shadow with small springs tickling the rocks. Down and down into the lowlands and valleys, and back home to East Tennessee. That was the autumn ritual.

The mountains hid old railroad beds, which later became hiking paths, so in many ways the hidden, ruined old roads followed the gradual devolution of those other relics of the mountains. There were many denizens of the mountains, however, who were not people. And Mellian and Silly-Delly came across a fair few on their travels: deer, foxes, elk, and the occasional black bear. Silly-Delly always became incredibly excited by the bears, and Mellian had to rein in the bot's heightened reactions so that the bears wouldn't grow too curious. *Especially*, she reflected, given the fact that they were all on the hunt for honey and other fine mountain wild treats. What neither of them realized was that there were other creatures living in those mountains...who never made themselves visible.

"We'll find honey on our own, and no need to follow any bears," she'd admonished Silly-Delly the last time they'd seen a bear. The bot had been crestfallen for days in disappointment.

Silly-Delly came in handy during the night, when they camped. Mellian had a small pup tent, easily carried either on her back or by Silly-Delly. The bot often stayed alert in the evenings, and occasionally halted during the hottest part of the day to recharge. That suited Mellian well; she preferred the dawn and late afternoon hikes, all the way until deep cobalt twilight. While the highlands were cooler than the lowlands, it could still get quite hot, and it wasn't safe to hike during high heat. Autumn provided Mellian with enough breathing room to do her work, while still offering great beauty and gentle warmth by day before the temperatures dropped beneath smears of starlight or wispy curls of mountain fog.

On this day, Mellian began to tire, while Silly-Delly remained charged and energetic. The sunlight kept Mellian going, though, and she was determined to find honey before nightfall. The flowers of the sourwood tree had long since dropped, their soporific scent a distant memory this time of year. Now the trees bore blades of scarlet as the leaves turned. Soon, all of those would drop, as would the remaining deciduous trees throughout the highlands. The diversity of trees here was unmatched, and rather than simple reds and golds of the Northeast, Southern Appalachia bore canopies of bronze, ruby, amber, chartreuse, burgundy, purple-green, and innumerable other hues. Mellian's vantage point afforded her that rainbow view, rolling and crinkling away into blue haze, the terpenes and isoprene watercolor wash of the trees smudging the boundary between land and sky like the moment between dreaming and waking. She could lose herself in that view, and the memories, and the pull of her heart and soul, swirled among the birds of prey circling among the updrafts...but Silly-Delly beeped.

She blinked and turned to look down at the gleaming bot. Its little eye lights glowed round and wide, or so they seemed to her.

"What is it, little fella?" she asked softly, darting her eyes among the foliage and all around. Not a single person could be seen anywhere...which was how she liked it up here, alone with her bot. Socializing was for the lowlands, to her way of thinking. Plenty of time for that later. She had a mission and she had her covenant with nature to abide by.

"I am picking up something," said Silly-Delly.

If she guessed correctly, the slight uptick in pitch of the bot's vocalizations meant it didn't know what that something *was*.

"People?"

Silly-Delly said, "No. Something else."

Mellian drew her mouth into a line. "Guess we'd better get away from the view and back into the brush," she said very quietly.

She stepped softly, slinking through the underbrush like a shadow, and when she walked like this, Silly-Delly knew to as well. Or, at any rate, as quietly as the little bot could; that kind of unit could mimic the sound of windblown leaves with its steps or rolls (depending on the terrain) if it had to. They reached a small stream, and Mellian could see that if they walked up it a bit, they'd be away from the road and out of sight of anyone, should there actually be people nearby.

And if it's a bear, well, we'll have to deal, she thought. She didn't dare bring up that to Silly-Delly. Now was not the time for excitement. Now was the time for stealth and watchfulness.

She spied a blood-red cluster of trees up above a small cascade upon golden stones, and for a moment she stood still at the water's edge and gazed up. This made her think of a wound: that the trees were blood, the stream a gash. But that moment vanished, for the light began to change oddly.

The red of the trees grew more vibrant, and their leaves shivered and whispered, and the light grew amber, glinting upon the edges of those fiery leaves, and sparkling upon the little freshet dashing down and down. The grove was of sourwood trees, Mellian knew instantly, and yet they were...different.

A subspecies? Her ecology mind puzzled a moment, but then she felt most drowsy, and she halted and leaned against one of their trunks. Deep cones of Eastern Hemlock poked up here and there between the scarlet canopy of sourwoods. She had never seen such vivid colors. And she had never encountered such perfect, ethereal light. Blinking, she looked down at her bot, and the bot looked up at her, and its little eyes whirred. It trembled, squat and low, as though shivering.

"What...is this place?" Mellian breathed.

By and by the glinting amber light bounced back and forth, the reflective golden glints flashing upon the scarlet leaves, and then some of these glints seemed to join together. Mellian felt dizzy, and yet so sleepy that she yawned. Then she felt a thrill of fear. The glints formed...a *person*. A person of *light*.

Silly-Delly let out a low, plaintive moan, which Mellian knew meant fear. She instinctively dropped her hand to the bot's dome head and stroked it. But she felt no small amount of mild terror herself. For the being of light approached them.

She stood frozen in place, and this being moved quite fast, as though it were diaphanous and drifted in the wind. There could be no way to outrun such a thing—if there had even been a path to run *on*, without slipping and sliding down the mountain. They were trapped.

The light of the being should have hurt to look upon, as it glowed nearly as brilliantly as the sun at the golden hour. But somehow, Mellian could gaze upon it, and she stared fully, absorbing all that light, her brain trying to comprehend.

"You—you're a *person*," she murmured.

Or at least, it was person shaped. It formed into something resembling a human, but some ancient, vestigial instinct in Mellian told her this was not a hominid. She'd heard legends of sasquatch-type creatures in the Appalachian woodlands, along their entire chain from Maine to Georgia. But she'd often scoffed at those, or grinned, depending upon who was doing the telling. No, this was something else. A being of pure light? She was not sure. And she was too stupefied by it now to try to escape.

It bore kind eyes: knowing eyes, deep amber in hue, and an upturned nose, and she thought she spied pointed ears. Something resembling a mouth formed, and...*smirked!* She blinked as it stood now so close to her that she could hear a strange sort of buzzing and rustling, as though the leaves bent in the down-sloping wind, or a hive of bees lived close by. It opened its mouth...

And it laughed!

All the buzzes and rustles funneled down into one word: "Hello!"

She stepped backward, and her booted heels struck Silly-Delly, who whirred and hooted like an excited owl.

"I...do not detect...life!" beeped the little bot.

The being then leaned down, seeming to place its hands upon its thighs to get a better look at the bot. The mouth in its face turned up in a grin, and its amber eyes shone. Mellian could discern no clothing; perhaps some covering, however...feathers? Scales? Some sort of pattern. No, she decided; it shifted like prominences on the sun, swirling and spiking out in little beams of light. She supposed that passed for clothing, but was not sure.

She was not sure of anything just then.

She *definitely* was not sure she wasn't hallucinating.

I did not eat the mushrooms on the trail. Her derailed thoughts managed to form some logic, but continually failed.

"No," said the being suddenly in its strange, buzzing voice, and she jumped.

She realized then that she had never responded to the thing before.

"Um...hello?" She wiped her hands on her pants; they were sticky from tree sap, from having pushed aside so many branches on the clogged mountainside. Then she held a hand out and said, "I'm Mellian."

The being beamed. The sounds of wind and bees spiraled out of its mouth, layered with additional sounds; clicks and sighs and perhaps the sound of the autumn wind in Fraser fir.

"That is what I am called," it finished.

"I...I don't know if I can...repeat that," she said, feeling foolish. "But this here's Silly-Delly, my honey bot."

The bot shimmied forth and scanned the thing.

"If this is life, it is not within my parameters to detect," the bot noted, its pitch high.

"It's life," Mellian breathed, facing the being. "Sorry, *you're* life."

"We are," said the being.

"W-we?" Mellian darted her eyes around, and then perceived a number of glowing lights, drifting slowly or darting about, and a bit of a chattering sound, as though the trees laughed at her and her bot. But no other beings approached. "Are you...are you fairies?" and a little bubble of a laugh flitted out of her mouth before she could stop it. "Too big, though. Fae?"

"What is a *fae?*"

Again the bemused expression on this brilliant person.

"Fae...well, they're mythical beings, magical." Mellian blinked several times. "Sorry, you're very...very bright."

At that, the being dimmed, like a star cooling. She could see then that it was tall, but not much taller than she; and the glints from its amber eyes seemed warm, if somehow mischievous.

Rustling: then, "Some of your kind might call me *spirit.* I have heard *haint.*"

Mellian burst out laughing, then clapped her hand over her mouth. She shook her head, giggling. "You're no mountain haint! A spirit? Well, I don't know. I'll just call you a fae. And maybe, since I can't pronounce your...name, I'll call you...*Fae.*"

The little arcs of light on Fae's body swirled. Softly, and with a more melodical voice, it said, "That is well. Come. You are seeking rest."

Mellian gazed down at Silly-Delly. "Well, that's pretty true. We were hoping to find some sourwood honey. There's plenty of the trees here, but the bees...I don't know."

An odd expression flickered across Fae's face. "Rest, then we shall see about more in the morning. Follow me."

So Mellian and Silly-Delly followed Fae past the scarlet grove of sourwood trees, and onto a path covered in golden beech leaves and through pungent firs and hemlocks. Their tracks slipped a bit on the fir and hemlock needles, mixed with pines, and away from the sourwood groves, deeper into shadow. The many lights whirled about them; and if Mellian stared straight ahead, she could swear she saw more of the fae walking beside them. But if she swiftly turned her head, they were gone, or merely the little spheres of light remained. She did that on one occasion, and when she looked straight ahead again, she gasped. For there, nestled under tall, dark conifers, their tops tinged golden from the sunset, a little log cabin rested. It was grey from many years, and upon its porch rested two old rocking chairs. In them sat the most wizened and ancient-looking two men Mellian had ever seen. She gasped.

"I...I know them!" she whispered.

Silly-Delly whistled. "These are far too old to be humans," the bot said. "You cannot know them. They are not in your records."

"Oh, you're so nosey!" laughed Mellian. "No, seriously...I had heard of them. How can they be real? How can they still be alive? They were gone before I was even—"

One of the old men stood and tipped his hat. She noticed then they both wore old, faded coveralls and worn straw hats, but the straw was also woven with something golden...not too dissimilar from the raiment of Fae. The men's skin creased into thousands of wrinkles, their rheumy-pale eyes glowing out, but they looked delighted. And she discovered they both had banjos by the side of their chairs.

"Hi, hello," she called, and she realized she sounded like a child, her voice broke so high.

The other man slapped his leg and glanced at his companion.

She could sense what they were going to say before they said it...because she had heard it many times as a child. An old, old recording her father had made before she'd been born, of two ancient relatives up in the mountains. They had said the same thing to her siblings in their childhood that they said to Mellian now:

"Why..." began the man on the left, all bones and old clothes and deeply grooved skin.

"Why, we're thy kinfolk!" finished the other.

And the first one wheezed, "Come! Sit a spell."

So Mellian approached and sat upon the topmost stair of the old, buckled porch. She knew this house must have been at least a hundred and fifty years old; maybe older. She sat rapt, staring at the two old men, who pulled up their banjos.

"What are they doing?" Silly-Delly asked.

Whistling, rattling cough-laughs erupted from both men.

"Cheeky booger, ain't he?" said the one on the left.

"Shore is," agreed the one on the right.

They both then nodded to Fae, who bowed almost imperceptibly to them.

"As they are your...kin," Fae said with some difficulty, "we will leave you to stay with them in their home tonight. In the morning, we will help you."

"I'm Mellian," and she beamed up at the two old gentlemen: their eyes glistened.

"We knowed ye," said the leftmost one. "But who's the little booger?"

Indignant chirping sounds erupted from the bot. "I am Syl-Del 5, and I am no booger! I am a condensation and collector bot."

Mellian turned her face away from her wee companion to avoid shouting with laughter.

"Dewdrop bot!" cried the rightmost elder. His brother nodded in agreement.

"And honey Fae," said the brother.

Mellian turned to look at Fae with questioning eyes. The being bowed to her, and all at once the light about the cabin took on the deep bronze of the last flash of setting sun. Mellian blinked, and Fae was gone. And now she could smell soup beans and cornbread and country ham sizzling, as a coil of blue smoke rose from the chimney pipe of the cabin. Somehow, in the time she'd spent turning to see Fae and then turning back around, the two old men had gone inside and prepared food. Silly-Delly climbed the steps awkwardly, until she reached down to pick up the bot.

"That is strange," said Silly-Delly.

"Um...which *part*?" she asked, her lips twitching.

"My time sensors seem to be malfunctioning. I cannot decipher the time of day...or even the year."

Mellian then felt incredibly drowsy as she entered the cabin, but was just hungry enough to remain awake. The men were nowhere to be seen inside. She found a little potbelly stove popping and crackling pleasantly. Silly-Delly rolled over to it, and Mellian laughed.

"Have you met a friend?" she teased.

If Silly-Delly could swear, certainly the trill escaping the bot would have singed Mellian's ears just then.

She turned to a small wooden table, bent with great age but gleaming from polish. Upon it there rested a big platter with a slice of country ham, curled at the edges from searing, a wedge of golden cornbread slathered with butter, and some fat brown beans in a bit of their broth. A tin cup sat full of cold mountain water.

"Thank...you?" she called out. No one answered her. Only she and Silly-Delly occupied the cabin, and in one corner a small bed stood, covered in a fancy ancient quilt.

She relished the food, savoring the salty goodness. The cold water coursed through her and she felt refreshed.

"Silly-Delly, I'm tired," she murmured, scuffing over to the bed.

"I do not particularly like this situation," huffed the bot.

"Maybe not," she yawned. "But I need sleep."

"I will keep watch."

"Mmm, good idea," agreed Mellian, but as soon as she crawled under the quilt, which smelled like honeysuckle and woodsmoke, she fell asleep.

She woke with a start. Silly-Delly was nudging her. She blinked and sat up, rubbed her eyes, and gazed into Silly-Delly's brilliant eye lights.

"What is it? You look worried," and she reached out to pat the bot.

"I am not worried. I am *concerned*, and if you must know, confused."

"How so?" She sniffed. "Do I smell coffee and biscuits?" she almost shouted, and she hopped out of bed. "Did they come and fix food while I was asleep?"

"They? The two quite strangely ancient humans on the porch, you mean?"

"Of course," and Mellian lifted from a plate a fluffy biscuit, steaming in the cool cabin, and took a bite. She moaned in delight. The coffee was bracing and hot, in the same tin cup her water had been in. She also found a little golden vial. Sniffing it, she sat upright. "Sourwood honey!"

Silly-Delly made a sound for all the world like a clearing of the throat.

"No one came inside to fix your food," said the bot.

Mellian, licking some of the drizzled honey, turned to stare at him. "What do you mean?"

"I was awake through the night, watching, as per the usual," said the bot stiffly. "I saw no one enter this cabin."

"They must've," said Mellian between chews. "What, did *you* fix all this?"

Silly-Delly spun around and around on the spot, eyes blazing green.

"I did *not*!"

Mellian felt befuddled but oddly happy, and unconcerned for the moment. She could not explain it to Silly-Delly. She felt at peace for the first time in a long time. She had been given comfort by family. She was not sure it mattered *how*.

She now felt alert and ready for anything, her hiking fatigue a distant memory, the aches in her joints gone...or at least silenced for the moment.

"Well, however they did it, I'll have to go and thank them," she said, pulling her pack upon her shoulders. It felt lighter, and yet it definitely contained something in it that it hadn't before. Before she could think on that too much, the door to the cabin opened, and in shone golden-pale light.

"Fae!" she and Silly-Delly cried in unison.

They both strolled out of the cabin to meet Fae directly. Mellian's two ancient cousins were nowhere to be found, their chairs empty; and there was no sign of their banjos, either.

"You needed honey," Fae said in its musical leaf-rustle voice. "Come with me!"

Puzzled, Mellian crinkled her brow at Silly-Delly, and the two of them followed Fae, who now was accompanied by many new bobbing lights, pale as the morning sun. They left the cabin and the evergreens, padding upon pine needles down to the hollow of vivid red autumn sourwood trees. Their tops were a haze of flickering lights...and constant humming.

"Bees!" cried Mellian. "A lot of bees. Maybe I should...hang back."

Fae turned and gazed into Mellian's eyes with its honey-hued ones. "They will not harm you; that is, if you do not harm them. We are the bee shepherds of this forest."

"Bee shepherds!" breathed Mellian.

And then she could suddenly see dozens more fae, fully formed, shimmering gold and white and silver under the brilliant scarlet sourwood leaves. There were gold and amber and copper pots beneath the trees, and above them great hives, from which dripped honey like liquid autumn morning light. There was a kind of music, but unlike any she had ever heard before. The fae people seemed to dance in a long, slow dance, and about them bees swirled joyfully. Mellian held her cheeks, and found them wet with tears.

"Have you...have you always been here?" she whispered.

Fae turned to her. "Long beyond memory and telling," and then the being gazed up into the morning blue sky, tinged with coral clouds. "We have made this a new home, as ours was...ruined."

"Oh," and Mellian reached out. Fae touched her extended hand and a tingle spread through her, and she could see...something. She did not understand what it was, but it saddened her deeply. And also, she thought back to the great mourning, the mountain tragedy, and Fae dipped its chin at her.

"Yes," said Fae. "So it was with your kind as well. Different, but the same."

"Yes. But you...you made something special here."

"And you will as well."

Mellian swallowed and her throat hurt. "I just...I just. I miss the old honey stands. Dad brought us up the road there. So close, so far; I don't know...I don't know when and where we are right now. But somehow, I feel...close to him now, close to that time. I can almost see it; I can almost see him holding up a jar of the honey with the comb in." She gazed through half-lidded eyes at the swirl of light beings and bees before her. A gold and crimson sight, drifting, dancing, very like the jars of honey and the scarlet apples on the roadside stands so long ago.

Silly-Delly nudged her, and she broke free of the reverie and looked down.

"Look!" cried the bot, and Mellian gasped.

All within its opened belly compartment, several capped golden vials rested perfectly.

"Oh, oh," she breathed. She jerked her head up, crying, "Thank y—" and she gasped again.

For Fae had vanished. All the light beings were gone; the urns were gone as well, and only the scarlet-leaved trees remained, with the musical little brook dancing between them.

She turned swiftly to Silly-Delly. "The cabin!"

They hurried back as best they could, dazzled by filtered shafts of morning sunshine, and to Mellian's great relief, they found the cabin...but no sign of Fae or any of its kind. She did see, by and by, two ancient brothers on rocking chairs, each holding banjos. They smiled at her.

"They've...they've gone," she said to them, approaching, her hands outstretched.

"They ain't gone," said the leftmost brother.

"They'll turn up again one day," agreed the rightmost brother.

"Come sit a spell," they said in unison, and, nodding to each other, they began to pick on their banjoes. Mellian sat on the topmost step, her heart full, her tears flowing. She didn't know when and how all of this was happening, but it didn't matter; she was at peace again. She could sense all her family about her, much as the fae themselves had darted to and fro. She thought if she just turned her head the right way, she might see them all. But she did not. She rested her hand on Silly-Delly's little dome head, and its eyes turned turquoise and it cooed.

And the two brothers sang:

The Dewdrop Bot and the Honey Fae
Strangers once, but not today
They follow Mellian, shining bright
And wander on the old Parkway.

The Dewdrop Bot and the Honey Fae
One's made of metal, the other sun's ray
They help make sure the bees sleep tight
And fetch their honey each new day.

The Dewdrop Bot and the Honey Fae
They dance all night and they sleep all day
They turn their eyes to the skies at night
And ponder on the Milky Way.

PUBLICATION HISTORY

"Elph and the Green Fairy"—original to this collection

"Too Late for Berries"—original to this collection

"A Break for Pastries"—original to this collection

"The Story Light"—original to this collection

"Falling Upward into Starlight" in the RISE anthology from Queer Sci-Fi (2023)

"A Swirl of Leaves and Sand" in Issue 8 of *Seaside Gothic* (October 2023)

"In the Wood of Frost and Shadow"—writing as J. Dianne Dotson, appeared in *Winter of Wonder 2022: Fauna* anthology from Cloaked Press

"All the Little Pollinators"—original to this collection

"Copper— BSFA Finalist—writing as Jendia Gammon, appeared in *Interzone* issue 295 (September 2023)

"Starry Eyes and Fireflies"—original to this collection

"The Theseus Stone" in *All Tomorrow's Futures: Fictions That Disrupt* CyberSalon Press Anthology (2024). Longlisted for the BSFA Award in Best Short Fiction

"Upon the Gloaming Hour" in *Seaside Gothic* Issue 11 (July 2024) Longlisted for the BSFA Award in Best Short Fiction

"Watercolors at the Edge"—original to this collection

"Star's End Gloaming"—original to this collection

"Ash and Violet"—original to this collection

"The Dewdrop Bot and the Honey Fae" in *To Appalachia with Love: Sci-Fi Anthology* benefiting Western North Carolina (November 2024). Longlisted for the BSFA Award in Best Short Fiction

"There Upon the Dark Branches"—original to this collection

"Opal World Frolic" in *Rhapsody of the Spheres* Third Flatiron Press anthology (2023)

"The Emerald Vault"—writing as J. Dianne Dotson, appeared in *Red Dwarfs Make the Best Homes* anthology (2022, edited by Seth Lukas Hynes)

ACKNOWLEDGMENTS

YOU HAVE PERMISSION TO daydream. I like to tell everyone this. I have always been known for the practice, sometimes indulging in it at impractical times. Then again, life has occasionally *been* impractical. And other times it's demanded logic. I have a degree in science, but my flights of fancy helped me to explain scientific concepts in new ways. That never limited my joy for writing the truly fantastical! Because when I daydream, and I spin new stories from my thoughts, I am always suggesting to myself, *why not?* Why not write about deep space libraries, San Francisco baker dogs, and cranky robots? Why not write about petulant fairies, a sorceress in the woods, or little elf in the aurora-gleaming snows of the far north? In a time of upheaval and uncertainty, let us remember the joy of story and the richness of possibility. And let's have *fun.*

I want to thank Christopher Payne of JournalStone and its imprint Trepidatio, as the first traditional publisher of my work in my first short story collection, *The Shadow Galaxy* (writing as J. Dianne Dotson), and for giving me a home again with *To Wonder and Starshine*, which is lighter in tone. I especially thank wondrous editor Scarlett R. Algee for believing in my words time and time again, and for championing this book. Many thanks to Mikio Murakami for this gorgeous cover, reflecting my love for Art Nouveau and Appalachia and whimsical science fiction.

Thank you to my children for their patience as I've tapped away on the keys at odd hours and, yes, during my bouts of daydreaming. And to their father for our long friendship and for his kindness. Thank you to my siblings for their constant and lifelong support for their baby sister, who always wanted to tag along with each of them despite our age gap. Thank you to Gareth L. Powell for steadfast love and support, and for his keen editing. Thank you to friends Pam

Magnus, Mya Duong, Helen Glynn Jones, Richard Czernik, Lee Campbell, Michael Mulhern, Vincent Cava, Dennis K. Crosby, Bonnie Burton, Robert Young, Jonathan Maberry, Adrian Tchaikovsky, KC Grifant, Kelly Varner, Danika Stone, Sarah L. Miles, P.A. Cornell, Andrew K. Clark, Lauren Warren, Sam Marshall, Ryka Aoki, and so many more wonderful people that I could certainly fill a small book with. And to all my readers, thank you.

In loving memory and gratitude for my parents and their own love for stories, and for letting me have a bit longer to daydream than could ever have been practical, for which I am eternally glad.

ABOUT THE AUTHOR

JENDIA GAMMON is a Nebula and BSFA Awards finalist author of fantasy, science fiction, horror, and thriller novels and short stories. She is also CEO of Roaring Spring Productions, LLC and Editor-in-Chief of its publishing imprint, Stars and Sabers Publishing. She has also written under the pen name J. Dianne Dotson. Born in Southern Appalachia, Jendia now lives in Los Angeles with her family.

Jendia conducts workshops and participates in panels on creative writing for conventions such as San Diego Comic-Con and Star Wars Celebration. She holds a degree in Ecology and Evolutionary Biology. Jendia is also a science writer and an artist.

www.ingramcontent.com/pod-product-compliance
Lightning Source LLC
Chambersburg PA
CBHW020646250626
47154CB00008B/2825